THE
Miracle Letters of T. Rimberg

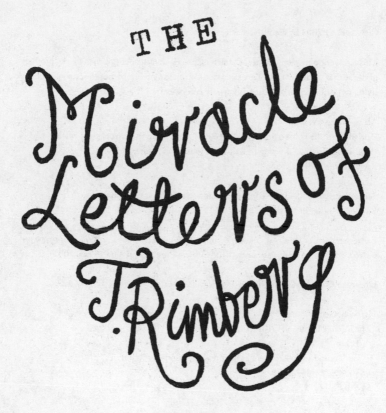

THE Miracle Letters of T. Rimberg

A Novel

Geoff Herbach

Three Rivers Press
New York

Published in the United States by Three Rivers Press, an imprint of the Crown
Publishing Group, a division of Random House, Inc., New York.
www.crownpublishing.com

Three Rivers Press and the Tugboat design are registered trademarks of
Random House, Inc.

Earlier versions of Letters 4, 5, and 6 originally appeared in *Workers Write! Tales from the
Cubicle,* edited by David LaBounty (Blue Cubicle Press LLC, Plano, Texas, 2005).

Library of Congress Cataloging-in-Publication Data

Herbach, Geoff.
  The miracle letters of T. Rimberg : a novel / Geoff Herbach. — 1st ed.
     p. cm.
  1. Fathers and sons—Fiction. 2. Depressed persons—Fiction. I. Title.
  PS3608.E725M57 2008
  813'.6—dc22

                          2007044762

ISBN 978-0-307-39637-2

Printed in the United States of America

Design by Elizabeth Van Itallie

10 9 8 7 6 5 4 3 2 1

First Edition

For my amazing parents

THE

Miracle Letters of T. Rimberg

Dear Council Members:

We have spoken about this occurrence, which has come to be known as the Miracle of I-43, and have agreed that it does, indeed, have a miraculous, although disputed, character. Immediately after the accident, the council asked me to prepare documentation on the primary actor in this occurrence, Mr. Theodore Rimberg. Due to Mr. Rimberg's compulsion over the past year to document his experiences himself, to write letters and journal entries, we have ample information. Enclosed with this correspondence you will find the documentation we created with his assistance.

Faye and I have tried to present as fair a representation of Mr. Rimberg as we can. From the conference call of August 23, you are aware that we have grown fond of him. With that said, we have not tried to color his story in a way that would make him appear more favorable to the council than he actually should. We have provided all of his letters, appropriate portions of his journal, and the entire interview transcript except that which is casual and superfluous.

In truth, Faye and I disagree about the inclusion of some of the information herein. While I feel it necessary to shine a light on Mr. Rimberg's many negatives, she would have preferred we focus entirely on his growth as a human being and his courageous acts. I'm afraid Faye is a bit displeased with me as I submit this examination. For that, I am sorry.

I want to be clear, however: Although Mr. Rimberg's story, personality, and many of his actions run counter to Church teaching, I find him to be a perfect vehicle for God's work. He is flawed. He is sinful. He is contrary. He is contrite. He is thoughtful. He is hopeful. He is human. I do not want to hide the fact of his humanity. The chips will fall where they may.

Perhaps this document, which is more of a history than a piece of persuasive writing, will be of little use to the council. If that is true, I hope it is at least of use to someone in the future.

No matter what, remember Mr. Rimberg's actions on the eighth of August. His courage and his accomplishments are at least commendable and at most miraculous. If only for that fact, we feel his story should be included in the occurrence's larger documentation.

Of course, we will treat any instruction you give us on this matter as binding and will end our promotion of Mr. Rimberg's cause with this letter.

Please forgive me if I am overstepping my office by being so forthright.

Faye and I sincerely appreciate your attention to Mr. Rimberg's case.

Yours in Christ,

Fr. Barry McGinn
Diocese of Green Bay

File: "Miracle of I-43"
Occurrence of August 8

Regarding Mr. Theodore Rimberg

August 28, 2005

Fr. Barry McGinn,
Diocese of Green Bay (Wisconsin)

Faye Sarni,
Diocese of Green Bay (Wisconsin)

Introduction

The following text is organized chronologically. Through interviews, letters, and journal entries, it covers Mr. Theodore Rimberg's life beginning one year ago, until August 22 of this year, two weeks after the accident.

My conversation with Mr. Rimberg begins two days after the accident, August 10, subsequent to my discovery of a backpack filled with his writings (spiral notebooks, the wire bindings replaced by yarn) at a Motel 6 outside Milwaukee, Wisconsin. Mr. Rimberg and I spent several hours every day for the next twelve days reviewing his letters and journal entries, reading them aloud, discussing the circumstances of his life at the time of their writing, and in general exploring his story and its connection to the accident. To create the overall narrative, I have inserted typed copies of the letters and journals between transcript sections at the point in the interview during which we read them aloud.

Final Note

Because of the length of the transcript and the speed with which I wanted to deliver the documentation to your offices, I asked my assistant to transcribe only his writings and his responses to my questions. Neither my questions nor my commentary are part of the record. I do have audio of the conversations, should you want to hear my portion. I apologize if the results of this decision prove confusing.

—Fr. Barry McGinn
August 27, 2005

Contents

Section I

Minneapolis

Day One (August 10, 2005):
Transcript 1

Note: Only Mr. Rimberg's responses were transcribed.

Yes. Ready. Go ahead, sir.

Okay, Father Barry it is.

I'm sorry, Father Barry. I don't remember who you are exactly. I remember you being around . . . was it yesterday?

Okay. Good. That was yesterday. I've been taking a lot of painkillers.

What do you want to know? I mean . . . I don't remember the accident. I can't help you with . . . I don't remember . . .

I'm sorry, you're more interested in *the rest*? Can you be—

You have my . . . Where did you get my backpack?

Letter 1
August 18, 2004

Dear Jesus,

I am drunk. I think I just got rich. My dad never came through for me in life, but looks like he's trying to make it up.

Not a chance. Not gonna work, Dad! Too late!

My wife took my kids, Jesus. She left me. My goddamn girlfriend left me, too! My job is nowhere, horror, dumbassed, dry eyes always dizzy at a damn computer. I don't care! I just don't care! I am drunk. Just peed in the yard! What do you think of that?

Here's hi-larious. Here's FUNNY. I'm going to commit suicide. Kill MySelf. I've thought about it for a long time and it is a great choice. Why not?

Are you laughing?

I'm not sad. Never felt better, which maybe you'd think would put me back in business (the life business). Wrong, Jesus!

I'm gonna do it. Why wouldn't I? Name a reason.

T. Rimberg

Day One:
Transcript 2

You have my permission to record.

I wrote to Jesus because I was drunk, I think.

Yes. I'm breathing. I'm glad you have my backpack. I'd be very worried if I thought it was still at the motel.

Okay. My name is Theodore Rimberg. Call me T. I don't know. That's what people have always called me. I'm used to it.

Date of birth, August 19, 1969. My permanent address is in Minneapolis, Minnesota. But I haven't really lived there for . . . I've been in Poland, mostly, for the last year. Now I am recuperating in a hospital in Green Bay, Wisconsin, after . . . an accident?

No sir . . . Father. I'm not Catholic. My wife, Mary Sheridan, grew up Catholic. My mother grew up Catholic, too. My dad—well, he lived as a Catholic during World War II. He was just a kid.

Yes, that's correct. Mary Sheridan is my *ex*-wife. I'm divorced.

Three children. A twelve-year-old boy and twin ten-year-old girls.

I wrote to . . . everybody. I don't know. One day, about a year ago, I started writing and I couldn't stop for months. My dad wrote stuff, too.

Yes. Dad is important. He was Jewish. I don't know why I wrote to Jesus. . . .

Because Dad inspired this. I got this . . . money. He's the reason I went to Europe.

Dad left when I was a kid, actually.

I was a tiny . . . I was a nine-year-old having heart attacks.

Letter 2
August 19, 2004

Dear David my "brother,"

I just tried calling. What in the hell is going on? You're never home or you don't pick up the phone. Aren't you home at two a.m.? I need to talk to you. I have some important news.

Shh. Listen.

Herbie, the Love Bug is a seriously fucked-up movie.

That's the truth. I hadn't seen *Herbie* since we were kids, David. Didn't we love it? I remember playing Herbie, running through ditches at Grandma's, honking, "spinning" our wheels in the gravel, pretending to do VW Bug wheelies, all in fast motion.

I'm very serious, David. Listen: It's a fucked-up movie.

Three days ago, I received *Herbie, the Love Bug* in the mail from Netflix. Had to be an accident. Never would have rented it. Charlie and the girls (my kids—you remember them?) like that new-style Disney crap (thanks to their mother) (no offense—I know you hold Mary in high regard), and I tried to show them *The Shaggy D.A.* last year and they were bored, pissing around, poking each other within ten minutes, paying no attention at all to *The Shaggy D.A.* You know why? *The Shaggy D.A.* contains no oversaturated colors or big-breasted mermaids to boil their desensitized brain chemicals. So *Herbie, the Love Bug*? I wouldn't have rented it.

But there it was, *Herbie, the Love Bug*, when I picked up the mail on Monday. And I was excited. It's my thirty-fifth birthday today. (You might remember?) Getting *Herbie* was like getting a birthday present a couple of days early. "This is just what I need," I said, "a little fun." But I was too beat after work to watch it, so I slept (poorly) and the next morning, Tuesday morning, I called in sick to work, cooked a big breakfast, brewed some coffee, and sat down to watch, totally psyched to walk down memory lane and ready to get cheered up.

Not a chance. Fucked up!

The truth: *Herbie, the Love Bug,* if you look past all the slapstick, hyperspeed racing scene, is a story about the need for sentient beings to be acknowledged, understood by their loved ones. There's this surreal montage, after Jim Douglas (Herbie's owner) buys a different, ostensibly faster, race car to replace Herbie, in which Herbie drives alone, dejected, through the wet and hazy streets of nighttime San Francisco (very noir) and haphazardly, as if drunk, weaves into a Chinese parade in Chinatown—amidst weird marching band music and muted firecracker explosions and dancing paper dragons—and finally moves ghostlike through wisps of yellow curling fog onto the Golden Gate Bridge, where he attempts to commit suicide by jumping over the railing (this is a VW Bug, remember). Luckily for the viewer, assuming the viewer is made of more hopeful stuff than me, Jim Douglas shows up in the nick of time to save Herbie (who actually ends up saving Jim as Jim's rescue attempt ends with him dangling from Herbie's bumper over San Francisco Bay).

But I am not that kind of viewer. I found myself cheering for Herbie's suicide attempt, David. The anthropomorphization of the VW Bug sank in deep for me, me being made of hopeless stuff, and I felt wholly in tune with the Bug's feelings of abandonment, his feelings of being misunderstood. Herbie didn't have a context in which to understand himself anymore—he was so alone—and since I live in the real world and not in a fictional one in which society accepts and eventually embraces the uncharacterizable (e.g., a skittish part-Jew who grew up underachieving in a small midwestern town who falls in love with not his wife), the impossible to label (e.g., a VW Bug with a heart, eyes, enormous desires), I felt the most appropriate and true-to-life ending of the story would be Herbie's successful annulment of his bitter, misbegotten life. And I'd started to think so only a third of the way through the actual movie.

And it was at that moment I began to seriously consider the annulment of my own (though I've had more serious fodder for suicidal thoughts in the last two days), a little more than a third of the way through my own actual life.

There you have it.

I'd like to discuss, so I'm sorry I'll be dead when you get this. You should rent *Herbie* anyway and see what you think.

You're not so bad, David. But you should answer your phone.

T.

P.S. Don't let Jared and Will watch *Herbie*. It's too much. You want to keep your boys off drugs, don't you? And if you're depressed yourself, don't do it.

Day One:
Transcript 3

David? I really don't like my brother . . . I mean didn't. Then.
Peace . . . Peace . . .

That's a meditation to help me be peaceful. It doesn't work.

I don't think so. I wasn't so weird as a kid. I just never felt . . . in
my skin. And I was sick. After Dad left, I developed a heart
condition, which was . . . not diagnosable. I thought I was dying
when I was nine. But I got along okay with other kids.

No, David didn't receive a package from Dad. Only me.

When I got the package? I thought it was a joke, maybe. Where
would my dad get all that money?

He was a diamond salesman, but . . . I don't think he ever sold
much. We lived in the middle of nowhere. There was no market.

Why are you asking me this stuff?

Southwestern Wisconsin. Dad said the location gave him easy
access to Milwaukee, Chicago, Green Bay, Minneapolis, Des

Moines. But I can't imagine he really . . . There were no four-lane highways to these places. It was a tiny town. I think he was hiding.

I don't know who he was hiding from.

I almost fell down. It was August, really hot on the front step. And I opened the mailbox . . . and there was the package . . . I ripped it open right away, because it looked so odd. It had foreign stamps, Swiss stamps . . . and I never got anything interesting at my mom's house.

Yes, I lived at Mom's alone.

My divorce was final in April. Mom went to the home in April, too.

Yes, I suppose that was lucky. Are you making a joke?

It wasn't the money so much . . . I really couldn't believe the check was real. It was . . . in the package . . . I hadn't seen Dad, you know, since 1979 . . . hadn't even heard from him . . . and there was his old man face. Pictures in Europe. I'd been to Antwerp once, too. Not with him. I recognized it a little.

One of the letters mentioned the money. It said something like, "Enjoy your inheritance, Theodore." You have the letters, right?

See, the letters were from Dad. But an inheritance implied that he was dead.

It did strike me. I received the package in August and the letters were—are—the letters are all dated December. Dated four months in the future.

It's right here—here. This one caught my eye, especially. December 7. I'm Theodore. Dad never called me T.

Um, sure. I'll read it.

Dear Theodore,

I wish you a Happy Hanukkah. A long time ago our ancestors, the Maccabees, began a rebellion to push foreigners out of Jerusalem (they weren't nice foreigners—they ran the place tough and were really mad at the Jews for failing to assimilate into Hellenistic culture). We killed lots of people, including many Jews who did not agree with us, and we got back our temple and we burned some oil that lasted eight days when it really shouldn't have. It was a miracle! The Maccabees, our forebears, they saved Judaism, but their brutality knew no bounds. All this violence at the center of a religious celebration? So strange, Theodore. But, not so strange if you think for two seconds.

December 7 was the first day of Hanukkah last year. My original plan when I read them was to kill myself on December 7.

No. Not revenge, exactly. I was sincere . . . in that I was . . . down in the dumps. I really wanted to die. Well, I didn't want to live. I mean, I was pretty unfocused about suicide—the actual act . . . at that point. I didn't get focused until . . . But I was . . . you know, my wife and kids . . . and I'd had an affair with this— this—and my job . . . and the money gave me . . . maybe revenge, okay. Except I didn't know who against.

Letter 3
August 19, 2004—
11:13 in the goddamn night.

Dear Dad,

I'm drunk off my ass! Happy? Happy Birthday me.

Second night in a row drunk. Okay?

You're dead, aren't you? Still, I'm writing you, you son-of-a-bitch. (No offense dead Grandma whom I never knew, if you're listening.) Where did you get this money, Dad? Why did you give it to me now? Where did you go? Mom could've used it, Dad. She's gone completely idiot from a disease that's eating her brain! Thank you so much. I live in her house, as you must know, since you sent this to my address. Mom's not home, Dad. She's in a nursing home, Dad. Do you know how the hell much she struggled with money after you bolted, Dad? And why give me the wad? Is there more? Did you give any to David? I just got off the phone with David and he didn't mention any surprise inheritance. He told me to stop calling. (Apparently I left ten messages on his machine in ten minutes.) He said it was too late to be calling. He called me a drunk! He's an asshole. David will not see a dime of this wad, and I hope he didn't get his own chunk. This is my money, Dad.

But, goddamn, I don't want your dirty money. Dirty Dirty Dirty.

What do you think about this? I'm going to use it to kill myself! I'm going to hire a sherpa and go up Mount Everest with the Wad and tie it all around my body and JUMP!

You don't believe me? How about a Hanukkah cliff dive? I'm going to do it. Check out the papers, because it's going to be a mess.

Thanks an ass-load, Dad! Abandoner. See you in hell, if it exists.

Your son,

T.

I'm not feeling very well. Could I lie down, Father? It's kind of hard to . . .

I'm very, very confused right now.

The coughing? Yeah. Yeah. My lungs are killing me.

No, not from the accident. I've had a pneumonia thing . . . for a long time.

I don't think the doctors exactly know what to do about it all, Father.

Sure, I'll call you Barry.

Maybe we can talk more tomorrow.

Okay. I'll do that. Sleep sounds good. See you tomorrow, Barry.

Thank you.

Reasons to do it:

1) Your life, how you live it, harms your children.
   a) How you work.
   b) Who you choose to love (no more Chelsea—hate her).
   c) How you spend your time (watching television while suffering jackass emotions) (pathetic).
   d) How you, when you lived with them, considered children and wife to be jail infrastructure.
   e) Your stupid potential.

2) How you don't live your life.
   a) No respect.
   b) No passion.
   c) No happiness, ever.
   d) Doing nothing to help yourself.
   e) No more good ideas—your relationship with Chelsea was an idea, which is further proof of your despicable character.

Possible:
Hang
Jump off cliff
Drive off cliff
Drive into tree
Buy gun (shoot self)
Buy pills
Rob bank and wait for cops, while acting crazy, with gun
Slit wrists—take a nice bath

Take bath with Mary's hair dryer
Disappear?

Where to do it? Travel? Maybe Washington, D.C., to make a political statement. About what? Nashville, TN, because once read that country music fosters suicidal notions (appropriate themes of marital shittiness, hardcore drinking, alienation from work). Nashville, TN: perfect place for underachiever to do dirty death dance. No—twang gives you headache.

Antwerp, Belgium, where Dad wrote on napkins?

Or check into a motel and take a bath with a hair dryer, not Mary's. Any motel. Tonight. Very soon.

Day Two:
Transcript 1

I'm ready. Go ahead.

Have you read everything? All the notebooks and everything in them?

Yes, I began carrying that backpack everywhere I went. It's been everyplace.

I wouldn't have called them visions. They were dreams, you know? I really wouldn't have called them visions then.

Maybe I'd call them visions, now. Yes, I would. I haven't had a dream in nine months.

I know exactly . . . the first was August 19 (my birthday and the day I wrote to Dad). The dreams didn't really get . . . huge until August 23. That day is a big day.

For one thing, it was the date of the last gassings at Auschwitz. 1944, sixtieth anniversary.

Yes. Gloomy. It was a gloomy time.

I don't know . . . maybe because I listened to the song "Vincent" by Don McLean about thirty times on my birthday. (Sung.) *Starry Starry Night* . . . You know it? Dad played it on an eight-track. He was fifty years old in 1979, but he had an eight-track. Old European Jewish Dad driving empty midwestern back roads listening to his eight-track.

I think that song affected my imagination.

Look in the journal. Not so clear at first.

Here. Nightmare one. I'll read it to you. *You are pressed into the doorway of a brick apartment building. There are searchlights in the clouds, searchlights dragging across buildings. It's like a Hollywood 1943 police search and they're looking for you. You can hear gunfire in the distance and explosions. You hunch down, so cold, bury your neck in your collar and there are boots marching on the street. You can't see the army or police, but you can hear the boots and hear gunfire. You haven't had dreams you remember in years.*

Yes. And then a little bit more every night.

August 23 was the first night I knew they were World War II dreams. It seemed reasonable, you know, given my father's reemergence into my . . . and his World War II history. That's the first time the little girl showed up, too.

Take action? You mean about the dreams? I didn't then. I thought they were just dreams. Take action how? I thought the dreams were symptomatic. War and annihilation dreams. They made sense.

I did figure out how to take action. Not for a while, though.

I didn't like my job.

Journal Entry,
August 23, 2004

Good T. Again drinking in the morning. Great work. You can't go to work. No more work.

Money Monkey.

Trained monkey.

One-trick pony. Don't know how to do anything except what you do at work, and you're not even sure what you do at work, but when you do it someone pays you.

Oh no, no skills. Can't build a house. Can't fix a car. Can barely cook. Barely clean. Lucky you can dress yourself (barely).

Dee-skilled.

Sit in front of computers under bright fluorescent lights that make you squint, walk around squinting. Squinty monkey wears pants and shirt and shoes.

Monkey. Jackass.

The money helped. I accepted it . . . because of what I was going to do with it.

I quit work on August 23. Same day big dreams came.

The job was—it was a symptom of . . . a manifestation of my lack of imagination, my total lack of courage.

Some stupid suburban office park. It was safe. Even when I wasn't suicidal I thought about driving off bridges on the way to work.

Marxist? I don't think so. I used the word . . . because it sounded funny to me. I thought I was funny. Used to.

I'm not a revolutionary.

Letter 4
August 23, 2004

Hello David,

I'm a Marxist! What do you think about that, you yuppie bullshitter? A naked Marxist!

Yes. What better way to celebrate the life and works of Karl Marx than to get totally naked in a staff meeting?

After calling you yesterday afternoon and you not listening to my complaints about work in modern times, man I was on fire, and I was feeling pretty free (I'm going to die!) and I was psyched to demonstrate how a dead man walking, with nothing to lose (not even a relationship with his brother who won't listen to him on the phone), could throw off the shackles big-time. My shackles were cotton Dockers and a light blue oxford.

After talking with you yesterday, I knew today was the day to part gloriously from the world of work.

So yesterday, in the evening, I got prepared for my glorious parting. I peered into my closet and chose the right outfit as I imagined my dumbstruck co-workers', mouths open, terrified eyes. I even went out and bought a new pair of shoes from Marshall Field's, the perfect pair of shoes (from the perfect salesgirl—whom I had sex with in a back room! On boxes of shoes!! Life is so good when you give up on it, David. You should kill yourself). Tasseled loafers.

And then today . . . Le Grande Act! (The Grand Act.) Check it out.

Our staff meeting this morning concerned a new service program introduced by corporate called "Service Starts with Me," or SSM. (Yes, the initials are suggestive of sadomasochism . . . no, apparently nobody thought of that.) When Dee Anne, my boring boss with a fucked-up 1987 hairdo, hit the SSM point on the agenda and began to speak in sincere terms about the need for every associate to adopt an SSM attitude and described how SSM will be the paradigm by which Carter Benefit Services will move from being a commodities-focused organization to being a customer service–focused organization, I slowly began to disrobe, starting with my tasseled loafers (ah yes! The first choice in naked meeting men's footwear—those bad boys slid right off). While she read the new standard script for answering phone calls—*Good morning. This is T. Rimberg of Carter Benefits. How may I help you, etc.*—I unbuckled my pants and pulled them slowly to my ankles, first one knee up then the other, along with my boxer shorts (yes, I went totally nude, after some deliberation—Karl Marx would have demanded that kind of commitment). The motion caught the attention of Jill Sonnenberg, who looked down and whispered, "Oh my god." Knowing it was do or don't, I jumped from my chair, kicking it back so it rolled hard against the wall. I stood up straight, unbuttoned the top button on my oxford and peeled it up and off, the tie still dangling at the neckline.

And nobody said a word. It was amazing, but just as I suspected, nobody pays any attention in goddamn staff meetings. Nobody other than Jill Sonnenberg and Dee Anne, who had been talking, even looked at me. Talk about worker alienation!

And there I stood, in a meeting of fourteen, hung in amber silence, arms outstretched, head cocked to the side like Jesus Christ himself, beatific semismile on my lips. And Alienated Michael Hendricks continued to doodle Rastafarians pulling long glass bong hits. And Alienated Terri Miller continued to zone out on the reflection on the tabletop and blink and nod as if she were listening. (Had she looked closely she would have seen my naked reflection framed by the great light window.) And Alienated Damian Stotz pretended to take notes. Alienated everyone else stared down at their agendas as if in deep thought over SSM until Dee Anne said, "What in the hell are you doing, T.?" her voice rising into the ether. And I didn't know how to respond and then everybody looked up, gasped, turned white or red, mouths open, quiet.

For ten more seconds I stood, frozen . . . a bit confused as to the next step a nude Marxist revolutionary should take. Then Hendricks started applauding, which startled me to action. I pulled on my pants, pulled my shirt back over my head, slipped my tasseleds back on, flipped a double bird, and ran the hell out of there.

Dee Anne screamed behind me: "I'm calling the police! You stop where you are!" But I kept running and went down the steps, through the lobby, and out into the brutal suburban light of the parking lot.

And I drove home to my empty house, sealed from the heat, not even kitty to greet me (did you know I left him with the kids when Mary asked me to go?), which might have been depressing, had my triumph not been so complete! And I holed up in my living room, expecting the cops to come take me. And I gripped a butter knife, which I was planning to charge them with, to see if they'd shoot me (a Marxist Martyr!).

But they didn't show up. Complete victory!

I am all air! This is the heady buzz the Communards must have felt in the early days of that great Paris Commune. What a glorious revolution. My days of laboring for the MAN are done! Karl Marx must be smiling, somewhere. Workers everywhere must be smiling.

Thank you, David. Have a GREAT day!

Day Two:
Transcript 3

I was jittery in the chair in front of the television in the middle of the night. I remember . . . the night I wrote that work letter to David. The night I left my job. Jittery. I'd gone to sleep, but then couldn't sleep because . . . I dreamt a whole story and woke up and then fell asleep again and the dream picked up right where . . . Finally, I woke up choking.

Yeah, there's a description of the dreams in the journal.

At least the door is open—so dark, those marching feet are soldiers. Spotlights strafing the sidewalk near you. You stand in terror, icy sweat, shaking. You bumble at the door, smash into the door, find the knob, turn it, and it opens, and you fall forward into a lobby, dark, no light except for gas light from the street and the strafing spots. Who is that little girl? She's in shadows. Eyes lit. You roll from your side onto your face and press yourself to the floor, the floor vibrating with sound from outside. It is black and white stone, the floor. Don't look at that girl. Don't look. You press yourself to the floor in the dark without breathing, cold stone. They're coming after you.

That's not it. I wasn't afraid the cops were coming for me because of getting naked at work. I didn't do that. I wanted to be a hero, maybe . . . but I made it up. Thought about it, but I didn't.

The letter was a lie. I didn't even go into my office that morning.

I drove to work sort of buzzed. I sat in the parking lot, sweating. Then I drove home.

No, I did not have sex with a salesgirl.

No, I didn't send the letter to my boss.

I didn't go back to work ever.

Letter 5
August 23, 2004

Dear Dee Anne,

You can't fire me. I'm not going to show up, which means I quit. I'm gone. Good riddance.

Hope your meatloaf Sundays continue to be as satisfying as you always professed (though I doubt they were satisfying). Quick point of advice: stop telling everybody every morning what you had for dinner the night before. Oh shit GOD did I hate Mondays—having to nod and smile and laugh at the appropriate laugh pauses in your stories about your daughters eating meatloaf, while all I wanted to do was put a stapler to my temple and slap it hard enough to end the misery. You are so boring. You lack any quality I would call interesting (except your hairstyle—*très* Glam Rock). Okay, you are great at your job (whatever that means). And I suppose you're a decent person. You're probably a good enough mother even, given your serious limitations, what you understand of the human condition (nothing). But, you're replicating yourself with these daughters. Three more little Dee Annes will eventually populate the cubicles of some financial services company in the Twin Cities. They will bring their husbands to your house each Sunday night and eat meatloaf. And they will head to the office every Monday with no story to tell, but they will tell it anyway, because they are soulless and totally boring. And there will be more suicides in the world. More and more. Jesus, Dee Anne. Listening to you killed me, Dee Anne . . . You're a good person, I guess . . . but is this what a decent life has to offer? Meatloaf dinners and fluorescent lighting? Is this really it?

What a fucking nightmare. Your poor kids. Your poor, poor kids.

Of course this is a suicide letter, Dee Anne. Of course it is. You kill me.

Take care!

T. Rimberg

Letter 6
August 23, 2004

Charlie, my son,

   What do you love best as an eleven-year-old? How can you do it forever? How can you make it the focus of your life? Do you think you'll major in theater in college? I'm sorry I didn't take you to auditions at the Children's Theater. I ran out of time. I ran out of gas. Don't ever focus on making a living. Make the life you want. Maybe you'll be a painter. (I'm looking at your fifth-grade self-portrait now—beautiful.) Be artistic. Don't worry about money. Don't have fear. Or if you do fear, make sure you disregard it and do what you need to do. Please, Charlie, go do what you love no matter what.

   Save the money you're going to get from me. Let that money protect you, so you don't worry. Go make a real life.

   I love you. I love you so much. I miss you. I am so sorry. I am so sorry.

   Your Dad

Day Two:
Transcript 4

Authenticity is what I wanted. I wanted to live for something.
(Of course I had no idea for what, after a failed attempt at a true
love affair, my big heroic act, which was actually an illicit
adulterous affair, which ended my sad marriage.) I mean . . .
That's what I want for my kids. Authenticity. I lived forever to
be alive . . . just to stay living, but not for anything . . . ate food
just to . . . eat.

Yes, I did just get dizzy.

Pale?

I'm not a big fan of . . . and talking about it . . . That was a
terrible accident, you know? My arm hurts in this stupid cast.

I'm tired, Barry. I'd like to stop.

Day Three:
Transcript 1

Yes, good morning.

Chipper? I am feeling better today—not so achy.

Only until ten. Shit . . . shoot. That's disappointing. I enjoy your company.

I really do.

I'm not normally such a sad schlump. Sorry about that.

No, no, no. No problem . . . I can read this afternoon while you're out.

You feel guilty? Did you have a Jewish parent, too?

Yeah, I'm funny. I'll do my best to be concise.

I knew the money was real when I quit my job. I wasn't risking anything when I quit.

I'd taken the check to the Wells Fargo branch in the neighborhood. I thought the check was fake, probably . . . I mean come on, you know? But . . . thought I should make sure. Then it wasn't fake, because the teller made a phone call and her eyeballs blew up and she took it, deposited it, and asked me about my other accounts, then she sent me to a cube in the corner, to the personal banker at the branch, Hector, who smiled across his whole bald head and shook my hand really hard. And then Hector insisted I make an appointment with a "wealth manager" in an office downtown, Linda, which I did from Hector's phone, and then I took the bus and took a fast elevator up to the twenty-third floor and walked into this— this office in a skyscraper down there and . . . Linda was so chipper. It was a lot of money. People don't have bank checks for that kind of money, except me, apparently. And I was fine with getting her help, too, you know, even if I don't necessarily like what Linda's about.

Oh. Well, I suppose I don't know what she's about. Linda has been great to me, really. She got an accountant set up. And I want to preserve as much as possible for the kids. Grow it for the kids. Linda helped me make trusts . . .

Protecting my kids. Those are big trusts, Barry. My kids have more money . . . not that money will protect them . . . Well, it sort of will. On one hand, anyway. Money goes a long way in this world. Huge insecurity for me . . . growing up . . . was fear of being poor . . . though we weren't that poor, I found out. My mother didn't tell the truth about money from Dad . . . I don't want to talk about Mom. My kids will not fear for their material security. This is the only way I can help them.

Letter 7
August 26, 2004

Dear Mom,

If you know about my death, if you're even cognizant, it isn't your fault. Okay? I mean, you did good work with not much in the way of resource. You made a decent home out of nothing. And look how David turned out. He sure is one of life's big winners, don't you think? That cat can really earn cash. And his wife is hot. You didn't have anything to do with me dying, Mom. You were David's mom, too, and he's great and his wife smells like expensive lotions. It just isn't your fault I'm dead.

Well, I kind of take that back.

In a sense it is your fault. Biology. Genetics.

I think I've read that depression is ninety percent inspiration and ten percent perspiration. And while I have perspired—yes, I fed the fire for years, muscles straining, mind trolling for the darker meaning up the silver clouds—I can't be blamed for the inspiration, can I? That's on you. I have to blame you for my biology. You did inspire me, breathed life into me, gave me my chemicals and my brain configuration and my combustible hardwiring, etc. For my biology, I must place responsibility squarely on your shoulders (and on Dad's—we can't forget).

But something else . . . you couldn't have known. You couldn't have thought straight about reproducing your own vulnerable infrastructure back in the sixties. You probably thought being blue was a personal problem. And, so, it was a thoughtless act, making me—thoughtless, because you couldn't have thought, "I don't want to make a sad child." You shouldn't blame yourself. I'm not going to blame you for anything. Biology is out of your control. So okay? Don't blame yourself, Mom.

And . . .

Do you remember Martha's Vineyard? You rented me a three-speed to use around the campground. But one day I biked out of there without letting you or David know. I was 13. And I biked along that busy country road, past the gray million-dollar clapboard homes, through the sea air, until I hit the quaint town there and pulled between parked sports cars to this ice cream shop and parked the yellow bike and bought a strawberry cheesecake ice cream on a waffle cone. Christ, was that good ice cream. Makes my mouth water thinking about it . . . There were so many opulent automobiles running slow down the central street of the little town: Beemers, Mercedes, Jags. Holy Christ. I have no idea what we were doing in Martha's Vineyard, except you had Kennedy fantasies, loved John F. Kennedy, who is also dead, by the way, and was then. And I felt like such a chump in all that wealth, us camping out at the crappy campground, driving cross-country in a Chevrolet Chevette (with which we pulled a camper? How?). Then I saw you drive down the town's main strip, your face white and blotched. You looked like an antelope with lions circling, just so scared, apparently for my sake. And when you drove past the other direction, I called out, "Mom." And you slammed on the brakes so some Richie Rich had to skid on his scooter not to hit you. And you jumped out of the Chevy in the middle of that busy street with all those Beemers and Mercedes honking at you and ran to me and hugged me, and Mom, I felt mortified and in love to see you and so rich to be cared about like that. I know you tried your best.

So, don't worry about it, you know? Don't blame yourself for this, if you're even cognizant. I existed because of you, and the good parts of my existence were because of you. I'm dead for other reasons. Be well. I love you. Charlie, Kara, and Sylvie love you, too.

Your son,

T.

Tick tock. Getting to ten. What do you want to know, Barry?

What?

I couldn't be with my kids. That's a different story.

No. No kids and I had money so I didn't have to go to work. Why not just die?

No family. No work. Should I watch cartoons and drink beer? Have some more nightmares so I'm awake for three a.m. infomercials about exercise equipment? That's a lonely—that's a lonely place . . . Should I think about Chelsea's long . . . her smile, her eyes . . . all gone? Why not cash it in?

I had the affair with Chelsea.

I told you I couldn't see the kids.

I really don't want to talk about it.

Mary wouldn't let me see the kids without her being there. Okay? Just . . . because.

Fine. Early in August Mary stopped by to drop off the kids— their Saturday with Dad! And I was completely wasted . . . It was ten a.m. I wanted to have one drink . . . to relax so I could enjoy being with them. I had maybe a hundred beers and Mary was extremely furious . . . about me being . . . and she worked with the lawyer . . . So, no kids. No more kids.

Listen. I know it's not . . . I think I have to . . . I'm going to grab a cup of . . . I have to run. You go to your meeting, Barry.

Things changed, yes. In the next day or so. Everything.

Letter 8
August 26, 2004

Dear Mary,

Listen. There's going to be a lot of talk. Who did what to whom, etc. Just to set the record straight, Mary (Mary . . . Mary . . . Do you know I love your name? I do. It is so solid. It is to be counted on. I love you.): I did it to you. I was the cause.

There is nothing you could've done to save us. Not paid me more attention. Not given me wider range to explore. You are the good one. I am the bad. And, you were right to kick me out. And . . . AND, you are not the cause of my death (though my inability to be a good husband and good father are parts of the calculation).

Feel free to photocopy this and send it to anybody who knows us.

Today, on the twenty-sixth day of August, in the year two thousand and four, I, T. Rimberg, say to you all, heareth this: My Sweet Wife Mary (divorced so not widowed) Has No Blame In My Death, Which Was Done Unto Me By Mine Own Hand, Thank You.

Yours truly,

T. Rimberg

Letter 9
August 26, 2004

Dear Mary,

I'm not bitter. If you ever get my other letter, I want you to know I am not bitter even though I said that Divorced So Not Widowed thing. And I would want you to be my widow. Not just my former wife. Oh Jesus. If I hadn't been such a fuck-up. I am a fuck-up, Mary. I got so lucky to find you and then fucked it all up . . . I fucked everything up.

I'm so sorry.

I do love you,

T.

Day Four:
Transcript 1

I had pancakes today for breakfast. I love Mrs. Butterworth. Is it even syrup? I don't know. It glistened in the sun.

Yes. A little will and testament in the journal. Here:

Item: The Chicken Dance is to be played at the funeral. Everyone in attendance is required to dance the Chicken Dance.

You know the Chicken Dance?

Of course. Green Bay weddings!

Item: My skull is to be cut in two, the top part polished a shiny white and used to serve mixed nuts on Super Bowl Sunday.

That's disgusting. No, I know.

I was ready to commit suicide on August 28, I think . . . I really thought so on August 27, before I had too much beer. But I had this dream that night, or in the morning. This dream was so real . . . I'd gotten into that apartment building and the war noise outside . . . I took the elevator . . . that little girl standing next to me, holding my hand . . . and I went up and into an apartment

on the fifth floor—we both did, me and that little girl—and my
dad was in the apartment standing at the window looking out at
Nazis marching on the street. And he was laughing . . . me and
the girl standing next to him . . . He was just . . . crazy . . . ha ha
ha ha . . . just dying at all this . . . troop movement, and
violence. The Nazis were marching deportees—Jews with the
Star of David sewn on their clothes, who were trying to carry
huge suitcases and their kids were trailing along behind . . .
tripping on dropped bags, skinning their knees and legs,
dragged up to their feet by guards . . . And my dad's laugh rang
out (now that I think about it, it was probably my grandfather,
not my dad—but I wouldn't have recognized that guy), and I
screamed, No! What are you doing? No! and then I woke up,
this scream in my throat, heart exploding, the walls and ceiling
collapsing in.

I jumped out of the bed and there was some light in my mom's
room, some morning light . . . I was still in my clothes from the
night before . . . the walls were coming down . . . I ran out of the
house . . . It was five a.m.

For a long time people I love . . . just atrophy. Mom going away.
And I lost Chelsea and Mary and my children. College friends—
gone. And before that my dad and with my dad—all the family I
might have known from him . . . My brother . . . I was
completely alone. But, because I jumped out of bed at the crack
of dawn . . .

Yes. I met Cranberry.

Dear Mrs. Carter,

I have a new friend named Cranberry and he thinks you suck. He should know—he finished high school a few months ago. He had a good English teacher who helped him plenty. Cranberry said you totally suck, Mrs. Carter. If you're still alive, I hope this letter finds you well, at least well enough to read, so you know how much me and Cranberry think you suck.

How does a high school English teacher grade a poem based on whether it rhymes or not? Have you ever heard of free verse, Mrs. Carter? It got popular among poets in 1920, maybe? That's right, FREE VERSE! You totally suck.

I thought my poems kicked ass when I was in high school. I'd write a poem and then jump up and down and pump my fist and shout out the window, "Fuckin A, you fuckers. Check this fucker out." And I thought, while I was writing them, I'd like to be a professional poetry writer. I'd jump around some more, tearing New Order posters off my bedroom wall. I thought, no matter how bad I hate my fuckface brother and my fuckface dad who disappeared, it doesn't matter as long as I have my poetry. I filled notebook after notebook with rocket fire word. And then you gave me a C and told me my poems were not very good, because they didn't rhyme. And then I sat in my basement for two months smoking weed, listening to the saddest music of all time, until my mom told me my b.o. was making her dry heave, which was eye-opening—I couldn't smell anything. And then I said fuck that noise, fuck everything.

I'm not a poetry writer anymore, Mrs. Carter. I sold my dick to the man, Mrs. Carter. I went to work at a large financial services company after college, where I still worked until a few weeks ago. And it was good times. During staff meetings I would think about overdosing on drugs or sometimes about sex, but mostly about overdosing on drugs. For years I sat there with the fluorescent lights burning a hole through my hair, staring at a computer. Then, a few weeks ago, during a staff meeting, I couldn't help it, I took off all my clothes, screamed and jumped around like a monkey on crack. I don't work there anymore. Maybe I'll write poetry. Thanks for your help.

Cranberry got kicked out of his house. Cranberry is a poet. I know he is and I'd give him an A, Mrs. Carter, even though he doesn't rhyme his shit. Cranberry is about imagination and intensity. I thought he was going to mug me when he accosted me early this morning, carrying a wad of balled-up notebook paper. I almost ran away from him, because he ran at me on the corner of Nicollet and 26th, shouting, "Hey you—Mister . . . wait," and I didn't know him and it was sort of dark still and his eyes were wild and red and he was sweating and he has a big mohawk, Mrs. Carter. He would mug you without thinking twice. I would, too. You suck so terribly, you poetry killer.

Cranberry got kicked out of his house yesterday. His mom has his CDs, Mrs. Carter. She also sucks. Do you know why she kicked him out of his house? He stopped obeying the house rules, which I told him was fair . . . he's nineteen. Do you know why he stopped obeying the house rules, Mrs. Carter? Cranberry loves his friends, especially one, who he told me is fat and sweet and smells like perfect sweet armpit and is on drugs and she makes Cranberry's young heart explode, because she is so desperate and sad and self-destructive.

Cranberry tried to help this friend. He stayed with her for a week, washing her fat and beautiful face with a washcloth, bringing her 20-ounce Sprites and roast beef sub sandwiches, buying her comic books at the store down the street—he stayed with her for a week without telling his mother, and remember his mother sucks. (So do you.) Then, while he was out buying the fat drug girl a Sprite a couple of evenings ago, she escaped her apartment, ran away.

Upon his return, Cranberry wandered through the apartment looking for the girl under beds, though he knew she could not fit there, and in closets. But she was gone. He stayed in her apartment waiting for her to come back, sitting on the couch made moist from her sweat and his tears, the sun setting. It tore him apart and she didn't come back, so he went home to his mother's, yesterday, and his mother kicked his ass right back out, because he hadn't called to tell her where he was. His mother has his CDs, Mrs. Carter. He slept in a park last night without his CDs. Do you know how Cranberry suffers?

You might remember my brother, David, Mrs. Carter. He never suffered. He had you for tenth-grade English a couple of years before I did. You gave him an A on his poetry. He rhymed *nose* with *toes* and *chose* and wrote about a rose and shows and waxed lyrically about the Black Crows, and apparently that shit blows you away. But I know the truth. David's poetry simply blows, as do you, you sucky old bitch. David is a lawyer now. He's unhappy and hates his pretty wife. Are you unhappy, Mrs. Carter? I should hope so.

Who doesn't suck? Cranberry. Cranberry has great panache. After he accosted me and read a poem instead of mugging me, a poem for which I paid him fifty dollars, a poem that detailed his fall from grace in beautiful symbolic language, I invited him to my house. He napped on my couch while I watched Montel, and he woke up crying for his fat friend on drugs, worried so much about her, his face green with fear, which broke my heart. He tried to call her. We drove by her apartment and she wasn't there. We could not find her, which made Cranberry dry heave like my mother when I smelled so bad back in high school.

We returned to my apartment and Cranberry wanted pizza.

We ordered a wonderful pizza from Fat Lorenzo's, a sausage one. The pizza didn't ever come. Cranberry, instead of calling back the pizza place, called 911. They wouldn't help us, even though our hunger was mounting. Cranberry called 911 again and again and again and again, screaming at the dispatcher about injustice. "No peace, no justice," he screamed (while I laughed and laughed). Eventually the dispatcher sent the police. Cranberry received a citation for unlawful use of the emergency system. I received a disorderly conduct citation for telling the cop he would die, which is true—it wasn't a threat, just a fact, Mrs. Carter. That cop will die. The cop didn't like my saying so—in fact he was really bent out of shape about it, told me to shut my goddamn trap, and then he booked us both. Luckily, me and Cranberry were especially polite at the station and there were no hard feelings. I paid our fines and everything's cool. On the way home we stopped by Fat Lorenzo's and ate a beautiful pizza.

Now we're sharing a bottle of Jack Daniel's, and we're both crying about life's terrible beauty.

That's good stuff, don't you think? Life as poetry.

But you couldn't know. You are a killer of good spirits. And you don't know shit about poetry.

Have I told you my wife left me? She took our kids. I'm glad she did, because I'd boinked another woman. My wife never knew about that, but she knew something real: T. Rimberg, who is me, is a gutless, soulless, middle-class fuckface. Who wants to be married to me? Answer: nobody. I had no poetry in my life. You took it away.

But now that I have Cranberry, I am a new man. Cranberry will be my administrative assistant. Cranberry will be my head of Research and Development. Cranberry will comb the cul-de-sacs of the Internet for the perfect contraption that will put me out of my misery. He understands me. He knows what I need to do.

I am going to die. No, not from cancer in 2017, but by my

own hand and soon and it will be beautiful. And just before Cranberry revs up whatever death contraption he finds in his research, I will write a beautiful rhyming poem with red Sharpie across my right thigh. It will say:

> *O' the verdant valleys of my tender youth*
> *O'er run by jack-o-lanterns' spilt seeds of mistruth!*
> *Then pack-ed was my craw with sweet burning pot*
> *So high, a balloon, so empty I got.*
> *And thus I shall shuck off my coil mortal*
> *And slide like greas-ed owl poop through portals*
> *Of deadly poesies and shit spun muck.*
> *Do you hear me Mrs. Carter?*
> *(Please hear me!) You suck.*

How you like them rhymes? I hate them. I hate myself. I hate you.

Hope this letter finds you well.

Sincerely,

T. Rimberg

Day Four:
Transcript 2

That's a terrible poem.

I was mean. I'd forgotten. Mrs. Carter doesn't deserve that.

I might still be mean, Barry. Don't know. I'm on sedatives.

Cranberry and I were taken to the police station, which was . . . great, I guess. We were taken and fined for a completely absurd act.

No. I don't write poetry.

Without Cranberry? I'd be dead. He might be, too, without me. Or maybe I wouldn't be dead, given my inability to die. I know this: without him I'd be very unhappy.

I didn't want him to stay with me. That first night, since he was so messed up, I told him to sleep in my mom's room. (I slept on the couch . . . I'm not interested in . . .)

The whole place smelled like a horse or something the next morning.

I asked him to leave late the next night. He said he had nowhere else to go. He shouted at me, "You want me to die in the fucking park?" Of course I didn't, but what responsibility did I have? And I sincerely did not want to spend the last days of my life worried about what the neighbor lady, one of my mom's friends . . . what Mrs. Peterson thought about me having a kid with a mohawk in the house. I honestly cared. Don't know why. So, I wanted Cranberry out. I told him he had to leave in the morning.

I woke up early. I went outside and had a cigarette. (Cranberry smoked, so I smoked his cigarettes.) I'd dreamt again of cowering in the corner of that apartment. Outside there were . . . volleys of machine-gun fire and people screaming and crying, and my dad (or dad-like guy) is at the window, laughing. And this little, vulnerable black-haired girl is next to me . . . and I could hear people crying for their children in the street. Sobbing for their poor kids . . . you know . . . "No—no . . . please—leave him alone . . ." And I woke up shaking . . . my kids and Cranberry's mom and how . . . how she should be protecting him, would be if she knew anything at all. Then all I could think . . . Cranberry . . . take this kid and keep him safe. This poor kid.

Yeah. Great trick for a suicidal—to protect someone else?

I feel fatherly toward him.

Journal Entry,
August 30, 2004

Document, the signing of which creates an hombre-to-hombre relationship between T. Rimberg and H. Cranberry Schmidt based on trust and the following duties:

1) Within the house H. Cranberry Schmidt is to:
   a) Use the Internet to research suicide machines.
   b) Wash his own dishes.
   c) Make his own meals (unless invited to join in a meal).
   d) Wash his own clothes.
   e) Act as assistant to T. Rimberg in any scheme created by T. Rimberg, regardless of the possible consequences to T. Rimberg.

2) Outside the house H. Cranberry Schmidt is to:
   a) Drive T. around, for T. is tired of driving.
   b) Help T. shop for groceries.
   c) Mow the lawn.
   d) Act as assistant to T. Rimberg in any scheme created by T. Rimberg, regardless of the possible consequences to T. Rimberg.

3) H. Cranberry Schmidt is never to claim to authorities or to Oprah or to Montel that T. Rimberg is in any way interested in him in a physical way, because that is not true and the thought thereof is enough to make T. desire to kick H. Cranberry Schmidt back out onto the mean streets immediately, where Cranberry, without his CDs and sweet, fat girlfriend, will likely die.

4) In return, T. will provide Cranberry housing, food, etc., pay all the bills and take Cranberry wherever he may go, and he won't, under any circumstances, refer to Cranberry as his Butler, which angers Cranberry greatly, although being called Cranberry does not anger Cranberry, which boggles T.'s mind, because Cranberry is a ridiculous name.

This agreement is binding until the time of T. Rimberg's death or whenever Cranberry wants to leave, which is fine by T., but T. won't kick him out unless Cranberry breaks with the binding rules set out herein. Amen.

Signed
T. Rimberg   H. Cranberry Schmidt

_____   _____

On this date: August 30, 2004

Day Four:
Transcript 3

The news? Nope. Haven't watched any television at all.

I am getting the letters and cards. I've read a couple.

No, I haven't read the newspaper. I'm reading a cookbook I found in the common room. It's a cookbook for . . . good Buddhist living, I suppose. Light eating . . . I want to be satisfied by not stuffing my face. For instance, as much as I love pancakes soaked in Mrs. Butterworth, eating all that makes me . . .

No, no television. How could I have seen CNN?

They're covering the accident? Do you mean my accident?

Patterns of light?

On the highway?

I don't know . . .

No.

Okay. Let's go. Let's get through this.

I'm not nervous. I'm fine.

Letter 11
September 1, 2004

Dear Caroline,

You were a helluva Prom Queen, did you know that? I mean, you were not only pretty, but you were just wonderful, too. So kind to everyone.

I am living now with a boy. He just graduated from high school, and he said that the Prom Queen at his school wasn't wonderful, but was just pretty, if you like Barbie dolls, which he doesn't. He calls Barbie plastic. That's no metaphor, Caroline. Barbie is literally made from plastic.

Do you like Barbie dolls?

I don't. I like real people, Caroline. You have a pointy nose and your eyes are sort of close set and your hair is mousy. This was in high school. I imagine you're even more like a real person, now, Caroline. Aging is hard on pretty people, I think. We're thirty-five. You know what will save you, even when you're ancient and your skin is saggy and your breasts hang down to your knees and your ass has gone flat and you can no longer hold your pee? You have the smile of a very good person. You have a big, pretty, glowing smile that makes you wonderful.

I've been thinking a lot about high school today. I'm stoned. I'm going to kill myself.

Best of luck.

T. Rimberg

Day Four:
Transcript 4

Cranberry opened up my worldview. At first he got me thinking about being a kid, in school. I'd been so obsessed with my dad and family, you know? I was almost done writing, I think, but then Cranberry reintroduced the outside world.

Kids are so vulnerable to the bullshit . . . bull crap adults spew at them . . . they believe a lot of it—but should they? Maybe they should believe it. I don't.

Right. I'm not that high functioning. Ha.

Kids are sensitive, though, and they feel happy and bad and evil and dirty and right and wrong from their hearts, which seems right. Really authentic. Like the Prom Queen . . . Cranberry was so offended by his Prom Queen. He pounded the table with his fist. "Why she gotta be so cold?" He cried about the Prom Queen (as if Prom Queens have a responsibility to be good to all the people at their schools—maybe they do).

Yeah, funny.

I played football, so I wrote the jerk coach. And then . . . I thought of everybody and Molly Fitzpatrick, who was my first love.

Yes, that Molly. Molly from the letter. Irish Catholic like you.

My intent was to write to everybody who affected me or I affected, to maybe lessen the damage to me and them. I really wanted to get to everybody.

Nasty? Most of the letters aren't, are they? I don't think so. I wanted to apologize.

Letter 12
September 2, 2004

Kurt O'Bannion, Football Coach.

You're really a fucking moron. Do you think it matters who wins a high school football game? Oh, that will change the world, you moron. Oh yes. And barking at us like a pro wrestler? "Get the lead out, you pussies!" You fucking jerk! Know what? While you were coaching the defense, all us running backs were planning to smoke weed after the game. We did smoke weed. Maybe a hundred pounds of weed, we got sooo high all the time. Might have something to do with how often we forgot the plays. Maybe if you hadn't been such a fuckface pro wrestler, we would've cared more. Maybe we would've won a few games here and there. Maybe I wouldn't be so depressed now, if I'd skipped out on all that weed smoking to be a stand-up, golden boy football player in high school (doesn't dope fuck up your brain structure?). (I'm totally high right now.) This is a suicide letter, you ass. Go have another Lite Beer. Moron.

T. Rimberg

Dear Sherri Staltz (if that's your name now—I assume you're married and whoever you're married to is very lucky),

I'm sorry I repeatedly touched your knees and legs backstage during the high school production of *Our Town*. As I was a football player and an egomaniac, I assumed you were as into me as I was into your knees and legs. Plus, your dress, the costume, was very pretty and you seemed perfect, and the truth is I wanted to sweep you away to some hot Florida beach and make love to you while Jan Hammer played beautiful synthesizer music in the background. Of course, I had a girlfriend and you were considered a geek by most of my friends, and thus I would never have had anything to do with you except in a clandestine, backstage kind of fashion. I was an idiot. And when you sobbed, "Stop it," I was really shocked, actually angered. And I called you a terrible name even though I knew you to be a really sweet person. Fuck me, huh? Seriously. Fuck me. I'm an ass. Don't worry, I'm going to fix this mess.

Please forgive me.

T. Rimberg

Letter 14
September 3, 2004

Dear Jennie Evans,

How are you? Are you married? I have kids, Jennie. Maybe you do, too.

And, I swear to God, in April of 1987, I did not dump the case of Michelob bottles on your front lawn because you narc'ed on the BEER BLAST at the quarry. I simply needed to get rid of the bottles before I got home, and your house happened to be on the way to Molly Fitzpatrick's house (my girlfriend at the time, you might remember). I'm intrigued, though, by your decision to narc on a party filled with jocks older than you and serious bitches. Small towns don't take to that kind of behavior very well, you know? And they made your life hell in high school, huh? Hope things got better. I assume they did. Can't get much worse than Todd Klein calling you a bitch and hacking tobacco spit on your locker every day.

Why did you do it? Were you morally against beer? Did you hope to gain something with the teachers? Letters of recommendation or something? Was it out of spite—the little power you could have over dumbassed upperclassmen? Were you trying to save lives, keep the drunk drivers off the road? It was just such an odd choice for a high school girl to make, you know? Do you ever think of it anymore, making that choice? Whatever—I didn't give a crap that you narc'ed on that party. Who fucking cares? Certainly not me. If you would've busted me, I would have kissed you on the lips. I'd like to right now— I'm excessively high.

I have kids and an ex-wife and I'm smoking pot with this kid who has eyes that sort of remind me of yours. Watery.

And I didn't mean to freak your shit out when I dumped the

Michelob bottles in the ditch in front of your house, and the fact that your dad caught me on the way back up the hill and asked me to roll down my window and then hit me in the head with the bottles should be enough payback, should even out the game, and I wouldn't have even cared he hit me in the head with bottles, might not even remember it, because I was drunk pretty often, even though I functioned all right . . . I might not even remember except when I realized whose house it was, I came in to apologize, to tell you it was a sincere accident, and you were totally sobbing in there, wrapped in a ball on the couch at eleven o'clock at night on a Saturday, even though you were sixteen. I guess you thought I was one of the good kids because I wasn't mean to you ever, and then I dumped those bottles, huh? It must have been a shock, like everybody in the whole world was out to get you. I swear to God I wasn't, and you were crying, and your dad, who was so angry when he hit me in the head with the bottles, started to breathe hard, too, his eyes all wet, and I can't fucking take it, Jennie. I can't.

Not that it matters now, but I wasn't dumping bottles to torture you. It was just to get rid of them so I didn't have Michelob bottles in the trunk of my mom's car.

God, all the terror in life, small and big, and you crying, and your dad . . . it makes me want to die, because I don't want to see my daughters ever cry like that. I don't want to see my daughters cry. I'm sorry.

T. Rimberg

Dear Charlie Hyde,

I hope this letter finds you alive. In first grade, when I punched you in the face after school, primarily because other kids mistreated you and I wanted to be like other kids, I felt very bad. When you were crying and saying you were going to tell your mom and you were bleeding in the snow and I was on top of you, pinning your arms down while I repeatedly punched you in the nose, I almost got sick. I cried at home afterward, but couldn't tell my mom why, because she would've taken me to your house to apologize, which I couldn't do—part of me wanted to kill you. I stayed in my bed for two days and wouldn't eat. My pillow got soaked with snot and tears, which is disgusting. You know, my dad ran away around that time and I was sad a lot. I think some of the rage and my ability to beat you stupid came from this. Also, nobody came over to my house when I was a kid because they were afraid of my brother, plus they didn't like me that much. But, that's no excuse and the fact is I'm very sorry, even though I hit you like that, I would rather have had you come over to my house to play with cars and have a snack or whatever, but instead I punched your poor little boy lights out, because other kids thought it appropriate to hate you, and I was sad and angry generally. You were an innocent bystander. Life is terrible. People are horrible and brutal. Charlie (that's my son's name, too), I hate that I punched you. I'm sorry.

T. Rimberg

Letter 16
September 3, 2004

Dearest Pastor Gergen,

I found your name on the Internet, which God hath made for us. Congratulations on your appointment. First English seems like a good church, Pastor. There were lots of wealthy congregants there in my time (small town wealthy, e.g., fat lawyers and funeral directors).

I need to tell you something.

When I was in grade school, after my father, a Jew, disappeared from the family, in a fit of Christian sentimentalism associated with the honey-soaked memories of her Catholic upbringing, my mother made me attend the summer camp run by your church, and something horrifying happened to me. Now, Pastor, you weren't the flock's shepherd at that time, so I don't blame you for the matter—in fact, Pastor Olmquist, whom I do blame, is likely dead (you'd know that better than me) (if so, may he rest in peace . . . after he pay-eth for the sins he did commit). But I wanted to bring this to your attention so that you could prevent similar malodorous treatments of the young-bodied and -minded in the present and future. Kids have got to be protected.

In the year nineteen hundred and eighty-one, a certain dim-bulbed twenty-something camp counselor by the name of Larry Graham—forgive him for he knew not what he did-eth and, really, he was a helluva nice guy—made a point of telling campers in the fifth-grade cabin that blasphemy is a Cardinal sin and Cardinal sins are those most terrible sins that cannot, will not be forgiven, under any circumstances, and even if God Himself feels like forgiving them, He won't because forgiving those would be breaking His law, going back on His word, so even if you are a decent person in every other way outside of your one instance of blasphemy, a Cardinal sin, God has no choice but to condemn you to eternal damnation and the searing fires that accompany it. When young Mr. Larry Graham was asked by one camper to define blasphemy so that his charges might avoid committing blasphemy, he said: "Uh, hmm. It's like if you said, 'I hate God.' "

"You just said it!" Tommy Banfield shouted.

"As an example!" Mr. Larry Graham retorted.

"Doesn't matter," I told him. "God can't forgive you. He probably wants to, but he can't."

Counselor Larry Graham turned an institutional white, and when we kept arguing, he marched us off into darkness to see The Man Himself, Pastor Olmquist, in order to get an official ruling on the matter.

It was ten p.m. So dark and misty that night, so the group campfire had been canceled and all of the cabins in the wood-chipped loop were dark, except our own. It was mighty dark and only Larry Graham had a flashlight, and we, all of us eleven years old mind you, followed Larry Graham so closely that we stepped on his sandaled feet and on each other's feet, because we were certain Satan lingered in the woods around us and God had forsaken us due to the blaspheming in our cabin, and we were practically hugging one another as we walked. Several of us whimpered. It was a brutal hike.

Pastor's cabin was two hundred yards into the woods off the loop and we could hear music as we approached—I recognize it as Chopin now. There were no lights on in that cabin, but Larry Graham still knocked on the door, and Pastor Olmquist whispered, Come in, and we did, and I think I remember the smell of whiskey in there, and Pastor sat alone in the almost-dark of a short-wicked kerosene lamp listening to music, handling God-only-knows what kind of emotional baggage.

Larry Graham asked him the question (as all of us huddled

behind him, cowering in the shadows): "If I say 'I hate God' as an example of blasphemy, have I committed blasphemy?"

Pastor Olmquist paused, lifted his eyes, shook his head almost imperceptibly, then said: "Do you believe in God, Larry?"

"Yes, sir. Yes, I believe."

"And what makes you believe in God, Larry?"

"Faith, sir. Faith is all we have."

"Then," said Pastor Olmquist, who was already seventy, I'd guess, and had flames of white hair that fired off the sides of his head, "let your faith be your guide. You know if you've committed that sin. You know in your soul. And so does God. How can I answer what is between you and God?"

"But I was trying to teach—"

"Poor Larry," Pastor said, shaking his head. "If you are unsure in your soul, perhaps you already have your answer."

"So . . . I . . . what . . ."

Pastor Olmquist pushed himself up from the table and whispered, pointing to the door, "Go on. You're violating curfew. Go."

We ran en masse from the cabin, all of us crying in the cold north wind and intensifying drizzle. And later, much later, I heard Counselor Larry Graham holding back sobs in his counselor bunk.

And that night, deeper into the night, Pastor Gergen, I heard a little voice in my head. I assume now it was my own treacherous subconscious, but was sure at the time it was Satan's tempting voice, rumbling deep, like the farts of the dead.

"*I hate . . . I hate . . . I hate . . . —Oh Satan be gone!—I hate . . . I hate . . .*" I fought and fought against thinking the words *I hate God*, and didn't sleep much the rest of the week, and didn't sleep much when I got home from camp either. In fact, I didn't sleep much for most of my sixth-grade year. I spent my energy working, working not to give in to Satan's prompts, not to finish that horrible sentence, not to suffer eternal damnation as poor, kind Larry Graham would. And the pressure in my soul built and built and built, and my sixth-grade studies suffered, and I did not partake in recess horseplay. I only sat in the grass, next to the redbrick school, straining with all my fiber not to say "*I hate God.*" But sometime late in spring, late in the night, hot tears running down my face, pressure radiating down my arms, my bedsheets twisted around me, soaked in sweat, I finally just let it rip: "I hate God!" I shouted, "I hate God!" and then I cried and missed a week of school. I was convinced I would burn in the eternal fires of Hell. I was never a real kid again.

Holy Christ, Pastor Gergen! The Very Reverend Pastor Olmquist committed a huge crime, don't you think? Who knows what became of poor Camp Counselor Larry Graham. Why didn't Reverend Olmquist absolve him, all of us?

I've spoken to other campers from my cabin that summer who had similar sixth-grade experiences, though less intense than mine. And mine, Pastor Gergen . . . mine. I had no father and a brother who detested me and a mother who had to work and work and work to keep food on the table. And then God hated me? Oh shit!

I don't know what I'm getting at exactly. I guess, just be careful. You bastards have a lot of power and I'm having terrible nightmares about Jews being murdered and I've had waking nightmares, my real life, in which I replay my own terrible, real, sins and I don't think I can be absolved and I want to get this shit off my chest, get rid of the brutality that has been done unto me and done by me, done unto everyone.

I have to go.

Don't bother writing back, as I'll be buried in some boneyard when you get this.

Thanks, Hank!

T. Rimberg

Day Four:
Transcript 5

I just get sick . . . I get overcome when I think about vulnerable kids, or people in general, getting hurt by . . . Using God as a weapon!

I don't know what I'm talking about. Do you know what I'm talking about?

It did start me thinking about God and religion . . . that stuff. The Lutheran letter opened up that topic. When I wrote to Jesus, I was just drunk.

Is that why you're talking to me, Barry? God?

You're wrong. Not everybody survived the accident. I remember.

Right. The driver didn't survive.

Letter 17
To the Manager, White Castle, St. Louis Park
September 4, 2004

Dear Sir or Madam:

Last June my son and I ate at your restaurant. Two lovely young women served us: a thin very blond girl with a nose ring and a short, stout African-American girl. The two were very sweet to my son and were having such a good time with one another, making jokes, singing to songs on the radio, it almost made me believe that race and class barriers in this country might one day be destroyed entirely. It was lovely to hear them laugh, like listening to celestial music, really. I ate thirteen sliders, had a great time with my kid, and went to bed so satisfied that night. I've often had a good time at your store. The teenagers who work there are always so happy. They make everyone else happy. Don't know how you do it. Keep up the good work.

Sincerely,

T. Rimberg

P.S. Any coupons should be forwarded to my wife and children at 3XXX Pleasant Ave., Minneapolis, MN 55408, as I have killed myself since writing this letter.

Day Five:
Transcript 1

Well . . . Uh, yeah . . . Okay—let me . . . I'm in love with love
. . . But I'm not a good partner to anyone . . . I wasn't faithful to
my wife.

Pray? No. Never. To whom would I address this prayer?

Oh yes, God!

I did pray once. I woke up with a dream. This little terrified girl
was next to me, holding my hand . . . I could hear the sound of a
train, this train beginning to roll, and I knew it was filled with
people all packed together so they couldn't breathe, and I cried,
Please, let everything not be real. But I knew it was real and God
couldn't make it go away. What does prayer have to do with love?

Connection to something sublime. So pretty. Well put, Father
Barry.

I'm not. Especially after the accident . . . especially after hearing
about these "patterns of light" yesterday . . . You think I might
be interested in God . . . Nope.

I'm learning to do light cooking. My body is a temple.

Yes, Mary did call.

I did speak with Charlie. It's been almost a year. I haven't called since I left Minneapolis.

It wasn't my intention, exactly. I mean I went to Europe planning not to come back, and then time passes and it becomes . . . embarrassing or terrifying. Weak stuff, I know.

It was good for me. Very strange after a year to hear Charlie's voice, although he wasn't exactly . . . I'd prefer, if it's okay . . .

My daughters wouldn't get on the phone. Can we talk about . . .

No, I didn't watch TV last night. I'm not interested in the patterns of light, and I'm not interested in God.

Actually, I'm not that interested in Europe, either.

Journal Entry,
September 6, 2004

This morning, kitchen sun, coffee, too tired. Slept through the night without dreaming about the apartment, because Chelsea . . . Chelsea in your dreams, which were soft dreams and you woke up and felt for her, then felt again her being away.

And the empty spot without Chelsea, the hole, made you mean.

Then Cranberry at the breakfast table, little asshole, wanted a haircut. You said you'd pay for it, but he refused, said it was dumb to pay someone. Everybody has scissors.

"I have no scissors," you told him.

He stood, walked to the cutlery block, pulled out a knife, and started sawing at his mohawk, glaring at you.

You said, "Goddamn it, stop." You stood, slammed a kitchen chair onto the floor, said: "Don't you ruin my mother's knife."

He dropped the knife on the counter, clattering. He moved to the chair, sat, face flushed. You scolded him for the knife disrespect.

"Jesus, so fucking sorry," he shouted.

"Don't shout," you shouted.

Moved to the utensil drawer. Told him that Dad purchased those knives in Chicago on a business trip, just before he left. That you remember him bringing them home. How much Mom loved those knives, said, "Oh what beautiful knives." So pleased with the measly gift. You took an old kitchen scissor out of the utensil drawer, which smelled moldy, unclean, smelled like Mom in the old people home. Your face got hot. Mom's gone.

"Where is your dad? Dead?" Cranberry asked.

"Have to spray down your hair. It's hard as rock."

Pulled the nozzle from the sink. Turned on the water. Sprayed his head.

"Is your dad dead?" he shouted, the noise of water splashing. His eyes closed tight. Water splashing on you and the floor.

"Maybe. Probably."

"If you don't know, he's not. Because you'd know. You'd sense it, man."

Didn't respond. Replaced the nozzle, picked up the scissors. Light from the window poured in. Mom complained about this morning light, standing at the counter, you and Charlie over early on a Saturday for sugar cereal Mary wouldn't allow. Most Minnesotans would kill for this exposure, Mom. Charlie crunching Frosted Flakes. Charlie's gone, too. You grabbed the front of Cranberry's sprayed-down head. "How short?"

"Inch, maybe. No, half inch, then it'll blend with the sides better. I'm going to make it purple. I had a dream about purple hair."

"Fine," you said, cutting, not good cutting, wincing at the cuts.

"Purple is *the* color. Where's your dad live, if he's not dead?" Cranberry asked, eyes shut tight.

"Somewhere. I got an inheritance from Europe." Grabbed the next few inches above CB's forehead, intending to mow the mohawk front to back.

"Inheritance? Then your dad's dead."

"No."

"What?" said Cranberry.

"I don't think so." You stopped cutting, thought.

"Inheritance? You don't think?"

"I don't think he's dead." The check and the letters and the postdating of the letters. And those pictures in Antwerp. And how he took you that time to Packer training camp. "I don't think so. But maybe by Hanukkah. He might not be dead, but by . . ." You cut slow, shearing the mohawk. Big, slow chops.

"I don't follow, man." Cranberry shifted, making you notch

to the scalp, to his skin, which scared you, a bolt of fear at seeing skin. You paused, then began cutting again.

And while cutting you thought: Dad's the only one. No David, who will not talk. No Mary, who divorced you for good reason. No Chelsea, who could not take you anymore. No kids, who live shielded from you under Mary's wing. No Mom, who isn't even Mom anymore. No one but dead Dad, who you loved so much, is left. "Cranberry?" you said.

"What?"

"Something . . ."

"What?"

"Just a second, I'm thinking."

"Thinking about what? Hey, stop cutting my hair. You're not paying—ow!"

"Do you have a passport?" you asked.

"What are you talking about?" he asked. "Stop cutting!"

Day Five:
Transcript 2

As soon as the decision was made. I made the decision to go find Dad in Belgium and it was like opening the front door to a blizzard. These dreams. There was Chelsea with her black hair all night long in that apartment . . . It all came blowing in. Not Chelsea's hair . . . Julia, too. Julia Hilfgott and Chelsea and rolling tanks, panzers I guess, and marching soldiers and all this furniture all over, which the little dream girl would smash . . . and the girl would chase me, crying out . . . and crying children outside and burning furnaces and smokestacks, and I was making love, or touching Chelsea . . . and my dad standing at the window . . .

Yes, I saw real objects. I saw real things in dreams. European furniture. Specific furniture. The little dream girl would sit in this chair in the corner eyeballing me . . . it was this chair made from a—a needlepoint. Like a medieval tapestry. Lady and the Unicorn . . .

You know it? How would you know that chair?

Oh, the tapestry. It's famous. Yes, that one.

The Unicorn symbolizes Christ's love? Are you kidding me?

The Lady is who?

These were Jews. You think they had some kind of Virgin Mary chair? That's a little parochial of you. I mean . . .? Jews for Jesus in Europe in 1942?

Wait . . . Wait . . . I think you're putting your own spin . . . Listen, Barry. Don't try to use me to prove a point. You can't make this point out of my story.

Fine.

The chair was real. I saw it later. In an Indian's house.

Indian from India, yes. In Antwerp.

We had to go to Europe.

I just did know. We had to go to Europe.

What am I doing here? I was half dead when we started talking, Barry, and now I'm afraid you're going to put me in some Jesus story. What am I doing here?

Why should I trust you?

Letter 18
September 14, 2004

Dear Cranberry,

I'm not going to call you Nick Kelly. You are a liar, but I will continue to hold up my end of the ruse. I will still call you Cranberry. But you should know: You've completely broken my trust.

Don't lie anymore, or I will throw you in the ocean. When my father left, I felt lost and hopeless, too, but I did not turn into a big fat whining liar.

I will throw you in the ocean, Cranberry. Do you understand me?

T.

Day Five:
Transcript 3

Preparations for Europe were made difficult because of Cranberry.

Of course I forgave him.

I trust Cranberry now. Of course.

I had no choice but to put my faith in the little jackass. There was no one else, Barry.

He did come through for me. I got lucky.

Not only did he lie, he acted like a brat. Before we left he refused to do anything. He wouldn't run errands. He wouldn't make phone calls. We had a contract. But he didn't want to go to Europe, didn't want to support me in my . . . situation, which was in breach of our contract. So finally I told him he could leave. But he didn't want to leave.

Poor kid. He had a lot of . . .

Nobody likes to get caught lying. He was afraid.

What lies? "My mom is a crack addict! Crack whore!" He said stuff like that all the time, which was partly why I felt the need to protect him. "Poor vulnerable kid. So smart for having grown up in such dire straits."

It didn't make sense that his crack whore mother kicked him out and kept his CDs. Why would she care if he was looking after a . . . another drug addict? I didn't have the best handle on what was happening. He lied and I believed him.

He claimed to have a passport, but would never get it, and the date of our departure was creeping up. It came down to this: I had to get his passport number to complete the purchase of the tickets. I'd already ordered them on the Internet, and I needed to plug his number into the computer.

Right. Why would the poor kid of a crack whore have a passport? Liar.

One afternoon I just lost my mind and screamed at him, and he cried and looked like he wanted to hit me, all red in the face with the new purple hair, and he dove into the couch and kicked the floor. A temper tantrum, like a whiny little . . . teenage cartoon character. So I told him I was going to take a drive in the car and he'd better get in with me, get in the car and direct me to his house or wherever he had his passport, or he'd better have cleared out of my place by the time I got back. He got in the car, sobbed the whole way, glared at me, but took me to his house in St. Paul.

A huge house. Summit Avenue.

I would love to know what percentage of the punk kids you see out on the street are actually wealthy. "I can go be as weird as I want to be because my mom won't let me starve if it really comes down to it."

No. His name is not Cranberry. His name is Nick Kelly.

He came back to the car, still crying, passport in his hand. I asked to look at it, saw his head in the picture, pre-mohawk, pre-punk, a preppie-looking Cranberry. He tried to tell me that the picture wasn't him and it wasn't his passport, that this passport belonged to the brother of a girl he once "did it" with. God. I'd already purchased a ticket for somebody named Cranberry, who is obviously fictional, and it's a nontransferable ticket, so I have to pay for a new one for Nick Kelly, and . . . I wasn't nice. I called Cranberry names. And I regret that . . . Cranberry is a good kid. His parents divorced when he was little and . . . This trip was, you know, amazing . . . I mean . . . Cranberry just needed to be fearless.

He wasn't fearless, but he faced his fear. He went.

I have a great deal of faith in him now. Yes.

Section II

Western Europe

Journal Entry,
September 15, 2004

You convinced yourself that love is gigantic, that love is everything, is to be pursued without regard for family or responsibility or anything, because it's so huge, so critical for humankind. Because, without it we are mere donkeys humping donkeys to produce another generation of jackasses. Love is huge, you decided. And it cannot be denied. Love is God. That's what you thought.

God loves David more and David loves no one.

And Chelsea. Shit. Love?

What were you thinking?

Day Six:
Transcript 1

People are *camping* at the crash site? That's very odd.

What do you think they'll see there?

Lights. You mean, what, streetlights?

They're pilgrims? Like buckle-hat Pilgrims? Are there Indians, too? Thankful feasts of turkey and squash?

I'm kidding. I am . . .

I am not laughing at them, Barry. No. Listen, I—I'm really not laughing. I have no grounds to . . . I just wonder if these people . . . if they were sitting here talking to me . . . would they think *me* capable of . . . I mean, I'm lucky in that I don't die very easily. But that's the only remarkable . . .

They're there for God, not for me. That's why you're here, too. For God.

Thanks. That's nice of you to say. I woke up worried you don't like me.

Because I told you I don't trust you.

How about let's get going? That would make me happy. Let's talk Europe.

Yes. I had the dreams every night at that point. Always. Unrelenting war.

During the days? I thought . . . well, I thought a lot about Dad . . . stuff we did when I was a kid. I also thought about the first time I went to Europe. Nineteen ninety. I was twenty-one.

I wasn't there for very long. Ten days only. Ten days completely upset my sense of self. Molly was the closest thing I had to home, sort of . . . most stable thing when I was a teenager.

I wrote her on the plane, yes.

Letter 19
September 16–17, 2004
Molly (née Fitzpatrick)
Presumably on Some Street
Likely in Chicago, Illinois

Dear Molly Fitzpatrick,

Where did you go? Why? Did you leave because you wanted something different than me in a larger sense, e.g., some young Irish guy, or did my actions that day prompt you to go? Good questions, don't you think? Perhaps I should have asked them fourteen years ago.

Well, I wouldn't be writing you, Molly Fitzpatrick (or whatever your married name is if you're married), except there were some signs I couldn't ignore—must've been the god of numbers (picture Charlton Heston) at work. The plane I just took from Minneapolis to Detroit was Northwest flight 616. Now I'm flying from Detroit to Amsterdam via KLM flight 1904 (yes, I'm in flight right now). If you put the flight numbers together—6161904—you get an important date: June 16, 1904. That's the day on which James Joyce's masterpiece *Ulysses* took place! I mean, remarkable, don't you think? How bizarre! And that date reminded me of you. I just had to write.

Oh, you probably don't get it. You're probably thinking: "Why does that date have any significance? What does James Joyce have to do with me?" Maybe you find this a little spooky—getting a letter from a boyfriend with whom you broke up (broke up—hmm . . . nothing official, was there? how about "from whom you disappeared?") fourteen years ago . . . am I right? Spooked?

Well, Molly, I think you should think twice before crumpling up this letter and tossing it aside as detritus from your past or the product of an unkempt mind (though perhaps it is—to be completely honest with you, I've killed myself since writing it). For the two of us, there's great significance to the date June 16, 1904. If there had never been a *Ulysses,* we might be together now, in the perfect marriage, perhaps. You know I always liked you. Don't you ever wonder, "What if?"

I'm sorry. I'm going to put words in your mouth.

"What if I didn't disappear?" says Molly Fitzpatrick.

It was June 15, 1990. We were between our sophomore and junior years of college. Really it's amazing we were still dating. What couple starts seeing one another during their junior year of high school, heads off to separate colleges in different states upon graduation, and keeps on trucking, keeps on keepin' on, keeps on being a couple? Sure, we had superb "see-you-after-not-seeing-you-for-three-months" sex. I mean the sex was short in duration (sorry), but it was fantastically energetic, right? And we were still dating.

And I was so dedicated to you, Molly. I was a damn hind-wagging Irish setter (not that I'm Irish—that's your gig) following you around with sad eyes, sniffing after you. And you liked having me around, apparently, which was enough to make you everything to me, absolutely everything. You slept with me ("In the biblical sense!" cries Charlton Heston) but kept an emotional distance, and that combination, I think, caused me to ache knees, hips, and elbows for you. Sometimes you'd give me moments of yourself, and you would call me (or not) late at night, in my dorm room, me waiting for you to call because you never picked up when I called. Oh God! I ached for you, but of course I couldn't trust you. Why wouldn't you pick up when I called?

That's right, Molly baby. I couldn't trust you; I couldn't believe you attended Notre Dame University without falling in love with some young Kennedy or having nasty one-night sex with some young O'Neil. I couldn't believe you wouldn't leave me. (You did leave me.) But you said on the phone when you did call: "I won't cheat. Stop it, T. I won't leave you." Still, my suspicious heart suspected you. And there we were in Dublin on June 15, 1990, sitting in a pub, on the goddamned Irish vacation we'd talked about since high school, drinking fat Guinness beers like we said we would, and you were morose, distant, sighing. Man!

"What's going on, Mol?" I asked.

"Nothing," you said. "Just tired from the flight."

"You don't seem happy," I said. "Aren't you happy? We're finally here. You get to show me the whole Fitzpatrick gig."

"I'm just tired, T."

"I was on the same flight. I've had the same schedule. I slept less than you. You were distant before we left, too."

"Jesus Christ," you hissed, attracting the attention of the old Irish men hunched over the dark-wood bar. "Can you leave me alone for one second? Have you ever heard of jet lag?"

I lifted my Guinness and swallowed big, five times, emptying the contents of the pint. My eyes watered, my throat stung. I looked at you; your dark eyes, Molly, and I saw nothing, no indication of your inner state—no love, no betrayal either—just flat dark disc eyes. And I needed something, some indication. So I threw it out there: "You don't love me anymore, do you? You're seeing some goddamn rich Kennedy son-of-a-bitch—"

"You're going to ruin this trip, too," you spat. "You are so ridiculously paranoid. You need professional help."

What did you mean by "ruin this trip, too"? What other trip had I ruined, Molly? We never really went on trips before. This is of some importance. I'm trying to sort things out before I'm gone (too late).

And we were yelling drunk, screaming drunk, making a big scene by the end of the night. Bar man said, "Get out of here," as we shouted at each other ("You are such a prick/bitch!" etc.). We kept screaming at each other in the street, people in the street screaming at us to be quiet. We hissed at each other going up the stairs in the bed and breakfast, other guests poking their heads from behind heavy wooden doors ("Shhh . . ."). We spat at each other in the bedroom (which we'd booked as T. and Molly Rimberg, to avoid any Catholic discomfort, to seem married, which broke my heart). And you passed out while I shouted at you and I barely slept, drunken sobbing the entire night. You slept fine, which still makes me angry.

Remembering that night, June 15, 1990, it seems impossible I liked you. There were good times, weren't there? Why was the fact you were Irish so important to me?

Holy shit, I'm uncomfortable on this airplane. Two Dutch guys are sitting in the seats next to me. They are so freaking tall, Molly, such Long Tall Dutchmen. In fact I'd say there are thirteen feet of Dutchman between me and the aisle. This complicates matters, matters being I have to take a whiz. What do you think? Is it wrong to pee into a cup on a plane next to two jolly giants? (They're laughing and laughing and laughing.)

According to the television screen hanging from the ceiling above me (which shows a map of our progress), we are about to leave North America behind. I can't see Minnesota on the map anymore (nor Wisconsin, where we grew up). The Midwest has disappeared! Good. Some home. No home to me. The great North Atlantic, colored royal blue in this televised facsimile, lies ahead. I'll let you know when I can see Ireland. Hey hey! The dinner cart is coming!

The smell of stale food is in the air. People are falling asleep. The movie *Die Another Day* plays on the screen in front of me, no map anymore. The Dutch guys are asleep. The son-of-a-bitch next to me has his feet draped across my lower legs. How can these Dutch stay sleeping through so many blinding movie explosions? I know how. The Dutch are comfortable on this plane taking them back to their families, comfortable on KLM, their airline, with their stewardesses, who are tall and beautiful and smile sweetly at the other Dutch people, and I suppose I will Die Another Day as will you, Molly, unless you're dead already. I don't know for certain you're alive. Here are the odds, though, if you're playing the odds . . . odds say I will die before you do.

I wish *Die Another Day* weren't on TV and I could keep track of our motion on the map. I really want to see Ireland on the horizon.

Okay! On June 16, 1990, you—I'll call you Mrs. Rimberg, because that's who you were supposed to be in that B&B (God, Molly Rimberg doesn't ring like Molly Fitzpatrick does it? Never mind. I'll call you Molly Fitzpatrick)—woke before I did. From the bed I watched you take off your pajamas. I watched you go to shower. I watched you come out of the bathroom, a light green towel wrapped around your head, and I was dying to make love to you (it wouldn't have taken long), but was so hurt, you know? Throughout our drunkenness and baroque emotion the night before, I'd done serious accounting and knew with utter certainty that when I'd accused you of sleeping with someone else ("You are fucking around on me!") or falling in love with someone else ("You can't live without an Irish husband, can you?!"), you'd done nothing but call me names ("Get off it, you psycho freak!") and yell and scream. You did not deny my accusations. So what was I to think? Ow . . . I'm hurting now just remembering!

You seemed disinclined to make love to me anyway, didn't want to like I did. (I would right now—I'm free to—my wife divorced me—too bad I'll be dead when you get this, huh?) But you weren't unpleasant, either, when you finally spoke.

I pretended sleep in that big feather bed as you motored around, water and shampoo smells trailing you, putting on makeup, drying your hair, filling the air with sweet berry lotion. Morning sun flooded the room, making the white curtains burst white. And finally, you leaned over me, already dressed, I'd watched you dress, all that sweetness seeping into my nose and eyes, and whispered in my ear, "T. I'm going down for breakfast. We're meeting Tim Boylen at ten. You should think about moving . . . I'm sorry about last night . . . I'm—"

"I'm not meeting fucking Tim Boylen!" I shouted, eyes no longer pretending sleep, eyes popping out of my skull, veins inflating in my forehead.

"Fine," you glared. "Do whatever you want." You grabbed your day bag and walked out of the room, slamming the wooden door as best you could. And you were gone.

I burst into tears before the door latched shut.

Tim Boylen . . . Molly . . . Oh . . . I sobbed for ten minutes straight, tears rolling down my cheeks, soaking into the feather pillows and feather bed. (Makes me suspect the cleanliness of B&Bs—all those tears, all that moisture-receptive material— seems like a breeding ground for disease.) You knew Tim from Notre Dame, of course, a real black-blooded Irish boy, and holy shit was I shaken. I wrapped your light green towel around my head and breathed you.

It took some time (snotty and tear-soaked), but eventually I couldn't stomach the passive stance I'd taken. I had to move: the pain and suffering and heartsickness and puppy love and adult hopes and all that sex I feared I'd never have again, it all swirled, a cyclone, lifting me from my wet, white feather cocoon, popping me into the air, wing-ed and beautiful—I would meet Tim Boylen with you! "I can make this right!" I peeled off the towel and hurtled out of bed in my boxer shorts and ran out of the room and down the hall and down the stairs and into the dining room, four tables of laughing tourists suddenly silent as a nearly naked T. flew into their midst.

You weren't there.

I begged the patrons' pardon, then ran to find the proprietor, and she told me you'd left without eating breakfast, but had left a note for me, presumably letting me know where you wanted to meet. She asked me to return to my room before reading the note. "You're . . .not quite dressed, are you?" she said, sweat beading on her brow.

"No. Sorry." I smiled, and I did smile sincerely. I felt great relief. Of course you wouldn't leave me behind without a plan to get me to you.

I walked back to the room, smiling warmly at the horrified guests plastered against the walls as I passed them. "It's okay," I told them. "She left me a note." Only a Japanese gentleman in a straw hat and woolen blazer smiled back at me, seemed to nod his agreement to what I said.

But he was wrong to agree, totally wrong, Molly, for here's what you wrote. Something like this:

I think it would be best if we spent the day apart. You really need to calm down. You're making me miserable and I'm afraid you'll embarrass me in front of Tim Boylen. His father owns a newspaper, T. I could get an internship from him next summer. Having you around right now is too risky. I really don't have a thing for Tim Boylen, so don't think this is about me spending time with him alone; it isn't. I really do love you, T. Let's meet back here for drinks tonight and start our vacation over. Okay? I've dreamed for two years of being here with you. Let's get it right.—Love, M.

What did you mean you didn't really have a thing for Tim Boylen? What were the implications there? Oh, I read between the lines, Molly. Did you sort of have a thing for him? Were there others you did, in fact, have a thing for? I sopped the feather bed with tears again for a while, then decided I would pursue my own bliss, my own destiny, perhaps my own Boylen-esque lover, and I jumped up, threw on my hippest, grungy, low-down clothes (which you hated), and bolted from the room, my face still red from weeping.

And here's where the date comes into play, Molly: The Japanese man in the hat and worn woolen blazer was waiting for me in the hall.

"Stephen Dedalus, I presume," he said.

"What?" I asked.

You know what? These Dutch stewardesses don't like me. They keep looking down their noses at me, smiling but not really. God they're beautiful. They're willow trees: tall, strong-trunked, arching arms set gentle against the artificial airplane breeze. No one could ever mistake me for Dutch. They are monumental. What a super-looking crew (a crew, much like the Rockettes, I could never join).

There! The blondest stewardess! She distinctly looked down her nose at me as she passed the row! God, it's not hard to see why Calvinists did so well in Holland. These would-be bombshells are the physical embodiment of the Calvinist reformation: certain of their salvation, suspicious of others, and utterly prim. How did these people create Amsterdam with all the sex and drugs? I think I'm going to smoke hash when I get there, Molly. No sex, though. I want to be true to my wife, though she divorced me, and true to my girlfriend, though she left me.

According to the TV screens, now back to mapping our progress, we're popping the cork on the upside-down bottle Greenland. And I can see it . . . Ireland on the horizon.

June 16, 1904, was, in fact, James Joyce's last day in Dublin in real life. He, a young twenty-something, left for the Continent after that. Never lived in Dublin again. But he dwelled on it—

not in a sentimental way. *Ulysses* is fiction but with a lot of fact in it. There's an older Jewish gentleman, Leopold Bloom (Jewish, sort of like me, right? I'm a semi-Semite), and he has a cheating wife, whom he loves entirely, Molly Bloom (Molly!), and then there's Stephen Dedalus (representative of Joyce himself), a young artsy-fart, dirty, unhappy, brilliant, hurtling without solution to the dissolution of his own parochial Irishness (as we hurtled to the end of Ireland as we knew it). Symbolically Dedalus and Bloom become one, or sort of, and, remember what the Japanese gentleman called me? Stephen Dedalus! Of course, I hadn't read the book.

"Call me Bloom," he went on to say. "Let's walk to the festivities together."

I had no clue what he was talking about but was in no position to disagree. I had nothing else to do! You'd left me stranded on the rocks.

Picture this (you probably even saw this): As I walked with the Japanese gentleman, "Bloom" (though I had my doubts as to the veracity of that name—I've always had fine instincts regarding truth), as we approached the River Liffey, sun high, along a winding major thoroughfare devoid of cars, we met other people dressed like Mr. Bloom: bespectacled and wrapped in woolen blazers. More people gathered with us . . . and more. Soon we waded in a swooning mass of straw hats, blazers, and others not dressed up and also many wildly hip women, beautiful young women carrying backpacks and books. This was a stunning sea of humanity.

My Mr. Bloom kept handing me a flask of whiskey as we walked. He talked about where we were going (Bloomsday celebrations—James Joyce–themed parties) and what we were doing (drinking hearty), and I nodded and smiled and said very little, hoping to keep my cover as this Stephen Dedalus so I could continue to float among the glories.

We came upon a tiny graveyard in the midst of Dublin. Buildings, three or four stories, old, gray, and also painted yellow and green and white, surrounded the dark green grass, the stone walls, the fallen headstones. The sun was high, abnormally warm for Dublin, apparently. My eyes ached from beer and light. At the gate a man stood in Charles Dickens–style undertaker's clothes. A coffin lay flat next to him. "What's up?" I asked My Mr. Bloom, feeling nervous, stomach washed in acid.

"Our first stop today, young Stephen, is to drink to the dead."

"Oh . . . okay . . ." I nodded.

And then from the undertaker reading from a big green book: *"Poor Dignam! His last lie on the earth in his wood box."* He pointed at the coffin (which, to be honest, was pretty small to be a real coffin—I didn't necessarily buy that there was a body in there, but, you know, I was hung over from Guinness, from fighting with you, from weeping sorrow all night while you slept and I had, by this point, consumed the equivalent of four or five shots of whiskey, so . . .). My head began to swim. I lost balance standing on the edge of that graveyard, sun bearing down, among laughing, half-drunk heads bobbing—the partying crowd.

And I began to have a vision, a hallucination: I saw you, Molly Fitzpatrick, my beloved girlfriend, my favorite journalism undergraduate, boxed in the little coffin next to the nineteenth-century undertaker. My response to this vision was normal at first—a heavy weight sinking deep, drowning, faintness. Yes, picturing you dead: silent, lying inanimate in the dark box nailed shut, your white skin whiter amidst all that blackness, your black hair thin showing white scalp underneath, your cheeks sunken, caverns underneath your eyes—it did cause my cheeks to pull down and my chin to quiver and tears to grow in my eyes. But then something shocking, so amazing: a light, elation. Actual light born in my dark middle. And this light rose in my chest, freedom from you, from waiting for your phone calls, spending every last cent on bus trips to you, wishing my last name began with Mc or O (considering taking your name when we married), picturing you kissing a tall red-haired rich boy on a crisp South Bend football day—freedom from you, Molly, from fear. This light expanded in my lungs and straightened my posture and continued to rise through my bronchial passages into my throat and through my voice box where it caused me to cry out like a shaker, "Oh God." And then light escaped, billowing, burping outward from between my lips, a bubble filled, it seemed, with ghost pictures of my real past that I do not know, and it floated ten feet above the crowd, Molly, not dangerous, a good light, riding heat inversions, rising from the woolly crowd, radiating the sun's heat back to it, until the light found a cooler place, perfect place, and became stationary, hovered. And there, as it hovered, it changed to crystal clear, the ghosts of my explicit past, colorful: a woman at an oval mirror combing thick brown-red hair, a man with a beard and a prayer shawl bending at the waist, and the bubble hovered and my eyes poured water from staring, from being astounded, Molly, from being overwhelmed. My Mr. Bloom asked, "Stephen . . . Stephen . . . Are you all right?" And I nodded because, Molly, these streams weren't sad streams riding down my face, this snot wasn't sad snot pouring from my nose. And then the light fell on a young woman underneath it, illuminating her utterly.

The young woman wore a blue tank top and had wild, curly hair tied back, and she held open a copy of that Big Green Book, and she called out, scanning the crowd with her eyes as she spoke, in response to the undertaker's reading: *"We come to bury Caesar . . . his ides of March or June. He doesn't know who is here or care . . ."* and when she stopped, Molly . . . the crowd fell silent around her, and she glowed in my bubble light and her eyes bounced across the crowd until they locked on me, the maker of light, and she paused and she whispered, breathless, barely audible, but I could hear: "Oh, you," and her eyes covered me, wrapped me up, and she stood there shaking her head slow, smiling, a Semitic smile, I knew it—ours was a preternatural recognition, Molly—I knew immediately this was something big, this Julia Hilfgott, whom I was about to meet.

And holy shit, you knew me as a skeptic, filled with mistrust. But holy shit there she was, Molly, Julia Hilfgott, who may have destroyed us, a Jewish girl. I told My Mr. Bloom, "I'm going over there."

"Of course, Stephen. I'll see you tonight."

And the Irish Sea parted, and I walked across it, Molly, the path opened through the braying crowd until Julia and I were face to face.

"Do you go to Brown, man?" she asked.

"No, Wisconsin."

"This is so fucked up," she said, sniffing, crinkling her nose, scrunching her dark brow. "I don't understand. I totally know you from someplace."

"I know," I said. "Should we go get a drink or . . ."

"Yes. Yes. Yes," she said.

And we walked away from the graveyard together, the crashing Irish Sea behind us swallowing the vision of you boxed in that coffin.

Did we walk together to the Promised Land? We did if our eventual arrival in Antwerp, Belgium, "The Jerusalem of Europe," counts for anything. But if by Promised Land you mean some sort of home—well, obviously not. I've never found home. But at least you were gone from my mind. (If only I could've kept you there.)

That's some serious stuff. Don't you think?

What were you doing with Tim Boylen all day?

We're almost to Europe now. I just pulled open the window shade a slice. The sun is making the entire sky the color of fresh-squeezed orange juice. We're flying into dawn. And, according to the screen, we're just about to cross Ireland.

In fact, there it is. And it really does look green. The sun is up enough. There is enough light and that country . . . your country, Molly—it is silent, unreal, beautiful.

Flying east through the night makes morning happen so fast. Dark Ireland sliding away. I'll be in Amsterdam in an hour.

You know, I had an amazing time that day. Unreal. There was a naturalness in my relationship to Julia Hilfgott that you and I never had. She and I were in sync. We sounded alike, although she grew up in a suburb of New York City. She'd just graduated from Brown, an English major like me. We had similar inflections, similar tastes in music and books (although at the time I'd never read *Ulysses*), a similar disregard for a neat appearance, similar senses of humor. And our bodies fit perfectly next to each other, after we'd had several drinks, lying in a park, spooning off our buzz. Did you see us lying together? Did you see us holding hands in the street? Did you know something was happening to me that day? Did you sense then that you and me inhabited new and different universes? Or did you know nothing at all and find yourself with Boylen and realize you belonged to him not me?

We're on final approach. The long tall Dutchman and his long tall friend are stretching, speaking funny (in Dutch), smiling, so happy. I guess they have kind eyes. In this light they look kind. And they're going home. They're rested. I have no skin on my ankle from the Dutchman's shoe tread, which rubbed on me all night. I am trying to go home, too, you know? But in Antwerp I'll be as much a stranger as I am everywhere. I'm looking for my dad, but I doubt he's there. And, no, Antwerp isn't my home just like you're not, and my god, Molly Fitzpatrick, I haven't slept a bit.

At eleven p.m. that June 16, the pub Julia and I were in closed. She said, "I'm taking a ferry to France in the morning. I have to catch the train to the ferry so early I didn't bother booking a room overnight. I don't want to be alone in the train station. Come with me."

"You want me to go to France?" I asked.

Julia paused. "I'm not staying in France. I'm going to Belgium. I'm visiting my aunt and uncle in Antwerp."

"You're kidding. Antwerp is where my dad was born, where his family lived."

Julia Hilfgott lit up, Molly. She lit up across her whole face, and I disappeared into her for a moment. I did. I knew for certain I belonged with her (for a moment). I knew positively I'd found my soul mate (for a moment). "You have got to come with me," she said.

"Yeah," I told her. "I know." And I did.

But Molly, I didn't leave you, did I? I didn't have the chance. Julia and I walked to the B&B. In that potential giant's night, and though I remember these enormous stars, *the heaventree of stars hung with humid nightblue fruit,* pregnant stars hovering in the black sky as we walked between street trees, I couldn't consider their metaphorical implications, their potential as guides to my correct life, to T. Rimberg's right life—you were on my mind. Our parting. The sad details of disunification played like video in my imagination: crying, last hugging, yelling, your terrible cold shoulders . . . How could I explain this to you, Molly? How could I tell you I was leaving? How could I leave Molly Fitzpatrick, whom I pursued so hard, whom I loved so hard, whom I called my soul mate for three years prior? This is the God's honest truth, Molly: as I walked with this Julia Hilfgott, I thought, "I can't. I can't. I can't do this to Molly. I can't hurt her. I can't leave her. I can't."

But the thoughts, they didn't matter. The thoughts were fruitless, weren't they?

My Mr. Bloom, the Japanese fellow, sat with others in a room off the entrance of the B&B. One man played piano and the others sang Irish tunes. I'd left Julia with her backpack on the front step, thought I'd come back to her in ten minutes to tell her I was staying with you. But as soon as I entered, My Mr. Bloom stood and said, "Stephen—your girl . . . your wife is gone."

"What?"

"She seemed upset and she left."

I ran to the room. Your bag, your clothes, your shoes, your brush, your everything was gone. I woke the proprietor, and she said you paid for the night then left. She said, "You should treat your wife better, Mr. Rimberg."

"Who?"

"You should treat YOUR WIFE better."

Then I ripped through all of my clothes and notebooks and even through my bathroom goods hoping to find a phone number to call Boylen or a number for the Cullens with whom we were staying in that little town on the ocean the next night. I didn't have numbers. You carried it all, Molly. You'd done all the organizing. (They were all your people.) I couldn't even remember the name of the ocean-side town. I tried calling your parents, though they hated me. They weren't home. My head filled with so much pressure . . . so much, it almost exploded. And then I thought: this is right . . . go with it, T.

And when I finally left the B&B, Julia Hilfgott was two blocks away, walking alone in the dark. I chased her, half sure things were falling in place.

"I thought you had second thoughts," she whispered when I caught her. Her eyes were red. She was shivering.

"No. Just shoring things up . . ."

And we walked on together, quiet. But the fucking Molly Fitzpatrick Irish termites . . . they were already eating me up.

I won't tell you much about Antwerp except to say those termites: our history, Molly, our mysterious parting, my excessive guilt, my distrust of anything that came naturally to me, but mostly my pining over you—it all killed this thing with Julia Hilfgott. Listen, Molly, don't take this too lightly, I'm serious, I saw myself in her and never saw that in anyone again until I met a woman who reminded me of her so much, but was adult and in the present, and she left me because I was married to someone else, someone like you. And what if I'd stayed with you? Disaster. And what if I'd stayed with Julia Hilfgott, whom I followed to Antwerp where my father's family comes from, both our families, Julia Hilfgott's and mine? All I could do in Antwerp was cry about you, think about you, fall back into this life, my life now . . . and my life is not good, Molly.

Julia Hilfgott didn't want me to leave Antwerp. I did leave (without saying goodbye).

What if James Joyce went back to Ireland after two weeks of exodus? What if Moses got homesick for Pharaoh? I imagine they'd have strung themselves up, too, eventually (picture Charlton Heston dangling from a tree).

And a year after I left Julia, me back in Madison, I met Mary Sheridan, who looks like you. A year later she was pregnant. (She's much nicer than you were, but still Irish and not like me.) Twelve years and three children later, she kicked me out of my house, which you would've done, too.

And now I'm divorced, alone, which I deserve, and I'm traveling back to Antwerp where I'm hoping to find something of my dad who is either dead or not . . . Antwerp, where I went with Julia Hilfgott . . . maybe I'll find something to give to my children, something HE, oh my absent father, did not give to me. I've never had a clue about home, and I'm tired of doing nothing but hurting my children, hurting my wife, hurting all people, though I suppose I'm writing you, Molly Fitzpatrick, my first love, my Irish obsession, to hurt you—not because the flights made the James Joyce date, I made that up, too, I'm a terrible liar. No, I don't want to hurt you, don't let this letter hurt you, and now I'm landing, the plane low over thin-slit canals that reflect the growing sun, and the day after I mail this letter to you, I'll be dead (so much for not hurting my children—at least I won't be able to again).

This is, after all, a suicide letter.

Where did you go that night? I'll never know. I never tried to find out.

I hope you are doing well, Molly, honest to God. I suppose you're a lawyer now. I really hope you're happy.

And I did love you, too much, in an immature way. I was really young—It doesn't matter . . . I'm sorry.

Here's Amsterdam. I'm going to smoke so much hash, Molly. Goodbye.

T.

Day Six:
Transcript 2

Destiny or happenstance? I guess that's the question. There was so much intensity right then. Really, I had three paths. One) I stay dedicated to Molly Fitzpatrick and meet her back at the bed and breakfast. I'd probably be a househusband living in the northern suburbs of Chicago (and suicidal). Two) I leave with Julia Hilfgott and follow that path, in which case . . . who knows? I might have Jewish kids, know who I am, and live in New Jersey—who knows what me and Julia would've decided? Would I have found a home with Julia? Three) I opt out, which is what I did. Hid away. I took a disconnected route, went back to Madison, didn't call Molly ever again, never contacted Julia, and began a whole new life, apart from everything. Destiny or random bounce of the pinball?

Of course you believe in destiny, Barry. God wouldn't fire us out into life and let us bounce around like pinballs. Clearly God wanted me to go back to Wisconsin to work in the deli at the student union.

Yes, I met my ex-wife at the student union.

It was intense, seeing Julia Hilfgott at that cemetery . . . I did see her explode in light. That was all true. I recognized her.

I saw her light up in Antwerp again. Julia clearly is . . . something. I'd be lost without her.

Right, Barry. God works in . . . God's big plan for me.

What do you think God's plan is for all the moms and kids dying in Iraq? How about that school terror thing in Russia? All those school kids herded into a gym and murdered, Barry? What was that? Does God plan all that terrible crap?

How is that disrespectful?

Journal Entry,
September 17, Schiphol, Amsterdam

Cranberry was angry we couldn't get seats together. But he came off the plane smiling, shaking his head. On his arm a young woman.

This woman, this Dutch, took us from the gate to a little café/casino with a smoking section near the gate. Cranberry is on his third cigarette already. He is golden, so much color in his face, staring at this girl. She is lanky and Dutch and in a business suit, and she can't take her eyes off Cranberry. What is she seeing? Her name is Kaatje.

Day Seven:
Transcript 1

The diocese is paying? What if I'm ready to leave? Will the diocese let me leave?

Thank God. Abducted by the Church. That would worry me. You guys have a jail?

Go ahead. I'm feeling good this morning. That secretary of yours . . .

Yeah, Faye! She brought me brownies and the original *Herbie, the Love Bug*. We watched it together.

Faye thought it was weird, definitely.

It was fun. I'm really feeling good this morning.

No better time than the present, Father B.

My first experience of Amsterdam was . . . I think it was colored by jet lag. I didn't sleep all night on the plane with those Dutch guys, and then I couldn't stay awake once we landed, especially after Cranberry went to meet with this girl, Kaatje. So I fell asleep

---

hard but then heard music, Chopin, a nocturne—this is so vivid—
someone playing a nocturne in the middle of the day, and I was in
or out of sleep, and this nocturne turned into a dream, which was a
quiet dream. I was in the apartment in the dream, nocturne
floating overhead, and I'm moving from one piece of furniture to
the next—really one piece of art to the next because the apartment
is filled with modern art, the furniture is modern art, modern
chandeliers hanging. Except there's that chair again, that Unicorn
and the Lady chair . . . and the little girl isn't around, which feels
lonely, because I expect her to be with me . . . and I'm looking at
this chair, the Unicorn and Lady chair, and something moves . . .
the woman moves, the stitched woman is moving . . . her head is
swaying on her long neck and her eyes are black and deep and her
black hair, dyed black like Chelsea's, slides out from under this . . .
this headdress . . . and the music, Chopin . . . and while I'm staring
at the tapestry woman moving, which—it is dawning on me—is
absolutely terrifying, the earth begins to rumble . . . shaking . . .
and the chandeliers are rattling and the plates in cupboards and
the sculpture is all moving from this intensifying vibration . . .
and I know that something terrible is coming. I scream.

Chelsea. I think . . . Chelsea is the tapestry woman, Barry. She's
stitched into a chair in my dreams and she's moving.

I felt this terror when I was in Antwerp before. Molly was gone
. . . like all of America gone . . . me haunted in Antwerp with
Julia. A fundamental hauntedness . . . I'm really wound into
something in Europe . . . wound into . . . I can't express it.

I woke from that dream by screaming and pinching myself, and I jumped out of bed and ran down the steps to the lobby. Down there an African woman was playing the Chopin nocturne on a piano. I had to cover my mouth because this . . . I was so . . . really seriously terrified . . . and Cranberry had gone off someplace with an unknown Dutch girl and Chelsea was a moving tapestry and this long African woman was playing Chopin . . .

It's like history isn't linear for me in Europe. I carry history . . . a somatic . . . cell level . . . connectedness. I mean you've read what I wrote about Antwerp, right?

And I remember thinking . . . I wrote something about it in the journal. Does God not want me here? Because that dream was scarier than any . . . was more real and . . .

Define God, Barry. Does he have a big Santa Claus beard? Paint a picture for me.

I don't think we're talking about the same thing.

You remind me of Chelsea . . . I mean . . . not exactly.

You just talk like her.

Journal Entry,
September 17, 2004,
After Dinner with Kaatje and Cranberry

They were so into each other, they forgot you were even there.
You stayed quiet, just watched. Cranberry and Kaatje
exchanging ions, wrapped in a field of gravity. And even though
they've known each other a day, you know they belong to one
another. And if they belong to one another, belong with each
other, then there is something larger than two individual human
animals, something that makes sense, creates connection and
sense, that makes it necessary for two people to be with one
another. Or you're crazy.

What if you never took a wrong path because those paths led
to Chelsea? What if the only wrong path you took was letting
her leave and that's when God started hating you?

Letter 20
September 18, 2004

Dear Chelsea, my love,

Is there a God? Something big outside our tiny lives, who drives us, individually, to make big choices for illogical reasons? If not, who is driving, Chels? Who is pumping the gas? My car is heading off a cliff. You should see my nightmares. (You're in them—you're made of thread on a chair or we're making love while hiding from soldiers.) Am I driving off a cliff, or am I being driven?

I had to believe in God when I met you. If you believe in soul mates and the transcendental horseshit that comes with that notion, you have to believe in God, or something. You have to believe there's a master plan. You have to fall on your knees and say thanks. You have to spread the word. You have to be a televangelist to the best of your abilities. You have to say to the camera, to the interviewer, "Oh Christ, yes, Bob! Look at me. Look at her. We're living proof! God exists, Bob. Look at us!"

First things first. If you're receiving this letter, the rumors are true. Believe the hype. I killed myself. (You are blameless . . . I love you.) And I wasn't going to write you, Chels. I promised myself I wouldn't, because I don't want to put any of this on you.

My promises? They aren't worth much. I'm writing.

I used to write you a lot. Lots of words. This is not that. I don't write e-mails anymore. I won't send you a postcard from Amsterdam (where I am now—sitting, on a very cold, gray day, in a stony square near some old palace, now art museum, dark clouds low over the buildings). I won't sit under fluorescent lights and write you a Post-it that says, "You know who loves you? You know. You know. You know," and put it on your computer at work—neither of us works there anymore. I won't send you fake memos, asking you to lunch, to coffee, to bed. Those days are gone.

Suicide letters. That's what I write. I'm writing hundreds, maybe thousands.

But this one is different. This one isn't about blame, Chels, because it's to you, and you didn't kill me. This suicide letter is about God and love, and I love you forever. It does, however, contain the most important information a suicide letter can (otherwise it's not much of a suicide letter): I am going to kill myself. Goodbye.

You're ambivalent. I know you wish you had faith, and you sort of envy and hate people of faith for their certainty and their idiocy. Maybe you don't want to talk about God these days like you did when we were together, God always on the tip of your tongue. I don't want to talk about God, either, never did, except I can't help it here at the end of my life. God is everywhere or nowhere. I am an atheist one moment and a pantheist the next. God God God. Today I think God exists.

What's my proof? Cranberry. Cranberry is my administrative assistant and butler (yes, butler).

Oh, Cranberry. He's lovely, had a powerful mohawk, now a short, purple coif. He is a poseur, a costume punk, the kind I could never be, though I wanted to have the guts, the panache (you have that). He stomped through the city in big boots and black pants, a scowl on his face, growling at people outside of sports bars, telling them to go back to the suburbs . . . He grew up rich (ha ha!) which, whether he admits it or not (and I am working on him to accept this fact), gives him freedom we of the middle class don't have. He is also tender and sensitive and a really beautiful poet. And Chelsea, he's in love, in beautiful, terrible love.

Of course a love like that makes me think of you.

On the plane over here, Cranberry and I sat separately. We booked our tickets late, and the flight was full. I spent the night next to two Dutch guys with long legs, crammed in the window seat, suffocating, unable to get up. I took this seat, because I thought it would be most comfortable, and I am the boss. Cranberry sat in the middle section of the DC-10. He sat in between two women, one tall but not so tall, the other a mother with a screaming baby on her lap, a newborn, a creature of God (a headache waiting to happen). But Cranberry had the best seat in the house, the best flight, even with the screaming and crying and burping provided by that poor, poor baby who couldn't possibly know how to deal with pressure changes and claustrophobia and bad food—which might also have been true of Cranberry, a poor baby at nineteen, innocent and unknowing, if something incredible hadn't happened to him.

The tall girl on his right had been visibly moved for the half-hour prior to takeoff. And moments after takeoff, she turned to Cranberry, eyes opened wide and filled with tears, and she shook her head, silent, spooking Cranberry. Then she whispered to him in her funny Swedish Chef Dutch accent, "I dreamt of you last night." The plane was still climbing hard and Cranberry was already having a mind-blowing life experience! (I'm a marvelous employer.)

Apparently Cranberry is susceptible to spiritual connection, magical connection, magical realism, ghosts, etc. . . . perhaps God. (I am, too, sometimes.) Immediately, Cranberry fell in deep love with the tall girl. Who could blame him? (Not me. I dreamt of you for years before we met, and you know what happened when we did.)

Could this girl, this long tall Dutch girl, be the special companion of Cranberry's soul? He thought a fat girl with multiple piercings who smelled like sausage was his soul mate before. But this feels different.

Do you know why Van Gogh started painting? He failed miserably as a preacher. Not because he couldn't communicate, but because he was too good at communicating what he saw as God's truth. Yes, Van Gogh drove his Belgian congregation crazy. Be beautiful! he would shout. You are beautiful! Made in God's image! And they were, this congregation, rather than turned on to God, seriously discomforted. Be beauty! something deep in them would cringe. They wanted solace for their gray days, not ecstatic messages, which had nothing to do with their shitty lives. They sat in the hard wood pews in black suits, hands hurting from long days of work, bleak light dim through colorless windows, stale air, gray faces, mouths downturned, elders growing in anger over this wacked-out Van Gogh, silently at first. The congregation eventually spoke. They said, "Van Gogh must go." And he was devastated, hysterically so, but undaunted. There are many paths to God. Van Gogh decided to spread his message of joy and beauty through painting, through creating amazing things. God on earth.

I was undaunted by the brutal realities of our relationship: my marriage, my kids, your evolving heart. You are beauty; you are God. I pursued you and continue to do so in many different ways.

There are many paths to Chelsea?

And of course, Van Gogh reminds me of me, except I have no talent and don't make anything. But when I see his swirling paintings, the fields of hay, the light, the texture, his bent bedroom, terrifying and beautiful, his swirling night sky, his vibrating self-portraits, I think of me. I, too, believed in beauty's power. I worked hard to demonstrate the vibrant, vibrating colors for you. So I didn't have a proper medium, didn't have the proper talent to make these perfect visions plain? I failed.

But talent doesn't matter much in the end. Live by beauty, die by it. Van Gogh painted *Starry Night*, then shot himself in the chest and died. And what about me? I made love to you, then hung myself in some empty meat locker in Poland (why not Poland?). Van Gogh and I have much in common.

Cranberry, with his purple hair and multihued, hayfield skin, is a breathing embodiment of Van Gogh's palette. I didn't come up with that. Kaatje did. She is twenty-three and works as a business consultant for a chain of hotels. On the plane, Kaatje looked at Cranberry, told him she dreamt about him, began to cry, then said, "You are like a Van Gogphk. (This, I swear, is how the Dutch say Van Gogh, and they should know.) Your pretty colors. So beautiful."

Cranberry knew Kaatje, too. He told her about his poetry, which, of late, revolves around a tree woman, who comes to him in his bedroom and makes plain his place in the world, in the universe. It's no lie. He has been writing weird woman poetry. He showed me some yesterday, after the plane, something about a tall Danish princess more willow than girl who inhabits his dreams and tells him to go to Europe. He's in Europe now. So that's something. Of course, I pointed out the Danish princess is not Dutch and, from the context of the poem, she is dead, lived centuries ago, and serves herself up only in the dreams of teen posers. Cranberry shouted, "I imagined Kaatje exactly!"

Cranberry often yells at me. He is filled with passion and energy. He has violent mood swings, which have nothing to do with the life of a middle-class adult and everything to do with teenage angst regarding his place in the universe, which I respect. I love that Cranberry.

This morning Kaatje called us from the lobby of the hotel. When we got to the lobby, she cupped Cranberry's purple head with her big hand and pressed him to her chest—Madonna and Child.

What was it in me that saw God in you? Why don't other people fall off cliffs like I do? Why is Cranberry able to pursue his bliss? Or will he fall off a cliff, too, regardless of the financial net provided by his parents? These are interesting questions.

Van Gogh had some kind of epilepsy that drove him wild. I have a hard time believing it was epilepsy, but what do I know? He tried to butcher Gauguin before he famously swacked off a piece of his own poor ear. Later, "for the good of all," he shot himself in the chest and died. I just learned this today at the Van Gogh Museum, which I visited with Cranberry and Kaatje.

Seeing the art and reading Van Gogh's story got to Cranberry. He got teary and told me not to kill myself, whispered that to me. And I thought, for a moment, perhaps I shouldn't. Look at these gorgeous, so completely alive paintings made by this freak! Why should I kill myself? Look at life! Then I got terribly depressed, facing fifty years of living, fifty years of paranoia and fear, fifty years of terrible nightmares, fifty years without you, and immediately sank, recommitted myself to the task at hand, then disappeared into darkness.

Van Gogh is my new hero. I had a great time in that museum, the Van Gogh Museum, the museum of my new hero. Van Gogh made me love you more, and you are life to me. I love life. I love you. You are gone.

In my nightmare last night, a recurring Nazi nightmare, you were suddenly next to me, not sewn into a tapestry but really next to me, and you were kissing my neck and then my mouth, and we touched hands then we made love and all the terror drained away and I was only with you.

God, Chelsea. I love you.

T.

That's why I want you to define what you mean by God. I didn't once think of a big bearded . . . flowing robe fellow . . . on a throne.

My God was more an ecstatic energy, a feeling. Think of homeless men in convenience stores talking about God.

You think God is comforting them? Is that Catholic theology?

Oh ho ho . . . nice. Yes, okay. Maybe I did conflate Chelsea and God. That's an interesting way of putting it, Barry. Sounds perverted.

I'm too literal? I've never been accused of that.

Her . . . intensity. Everything intense. Big hands and eyes and shoulders . . . She washed over me, filled me. I suppose she gave me a notion of how to live? She was a guide. She was all action, which was very sexy. Incredibly sexy.

I don't know that I do know the difference between a sexual and a spiritual experience. Being with her felt like a spiritual experience.

I'm surprised you're entertaining this at all. I was a married man having an affair, you know? Don't you condemn that?

It is complicated.

Right. You're right. Not that complicated.

Letter 21
September 18, 2004

Dear Vincent Van Gogh,

I went to your museum today and had a beautiful time. Why do you sound so happy in your letters to Theo? You weren't happy, were you? I'm not ever happy, and yet, I think, in all of the letters I write, I sound quite happy. I write suicide letters, Vincent!

In one of the translated letters I read, you suggest Theo should smoke a pipe, as it is a cure for the blues. You say you happen to have the blues now and then. So you smoke a pipe.

We are so much alike. Except I think you were a good person. I am not a good person.

I'm going to smoke hashish. What did you put in your pipe, Vincent?

I'm sorry you had the blues.

Your great admirer,

T. Rimberg

Letter 22
September 18, 2004

Dear Chelsea,

I only stopped writing you an hour ago. I have stopped in a "coffee" house. Cranberry wasn't in the hotel room and he left no note. I can only assume he is with his new love, Kaatje. And so I am alone—or sort of alone, I've been talking to people around me a little.

Why am I in Europe? To find my dad. Cranberry is distracting.

Yes, here I am, on another continent and in a "coffee" house where the hash smoke is thick and sweet. I've been told it's Moroccan, and it is dark, oily, beautiful. It smells organic and sweet, and it smells like you.

There are people on either side of me, sitting with other people, smoking and talking quietly. My energy is high. I am sort of sunnily suicidal today, and this is a very quiet, dark place. No light is let in through the windows, and the lights in here are dim, casting dark orange on dark wood, and there's no music playing, only people murmuring, whispering, many of them in wool coats, because it's cold. Where's the pot laughter? Where's the Marley music? Come on! There are Rasta flags all around me and pictures of Rastafarians and there are some Rastafarian types sitting in this café, but they just whisper to the German and Dutch and English intellectuals while they smoke their ganja. Nothing is light.

I'm drinking tea.

You would love it here. You like pot. I became afraid of pot, as you know. Remember when we smoked pot? You had it stashed in your panty drawer for God knows how long and then we smoked it out of that one-hitter pipe, sitting cross-legged on the beige carpet of your duplex living room. The one-hitter, the heat, burned my throat and made me hack big puffy smoke coughs, while you laughed and laughed, sitting on the floor of your tiny living room, folding over laughing at my coughing tears. We were listening to Coltrane, Coltrane—what a funny name. You got calm when I stopped choking, touched my cheek with your big, beautiful, electric hand, told me you loved me desperately. But then my heart raced and I began to sweat, and then I felt the panic, and you asked if I was okay, which I was not, then I ran out of your house, got in my car, and drove straight north twenty miles, up to Lino Lakes to a gas station, where I stayed for three hours, because I couldn't stay at your house, on fire high. My car was parked in your driveway and I knew Mary would drive by your house, even though your house was miles from my family's house. I just knew Mary would drive by.

Oh shit, Chelsea. I wish I hadn't driven away, showing you that. I'm so sorry I was afraid to be caught with you.

You wouldn't speak to me at the office on Monday (though I'd e-mailed my apologies over the weekend and you'd responded, "It's fine."). You wouldn't speak to me for several days after that and I didn't know why, except I guessed you thought I couldn't hold my weed, which seemed ridiculous, because you gave me drugs and I acted weird, which is how people act on drugs. So what if I drove to some North Suburb and parked my car at a Super America where I ate three horrible rotisserie hot dogs and a terrifying Mex wrap called a Taquito? Of course I did that. I was on drugs, which you gave me.

But now, of course, it occurs to me that you understood something about my wife Mary and what she meant to me. What you understood at that moment was: T. is not in this with me for the long haul because he ran away to Lino Lakes to hide his car from his wife.

I'm so sorry. I made no mistakes in my whole life, because all choices led to you. But then I didn't choose you. How could God have let this happen?

I shouldn't smoke hashish. But it is too late. I crumbled this oily, Moroccan stuff I got from the bar into tobacco, and the guy next to me rolled it up in a cigarette, smiling at me, because I can't roll a joint right and now I am getting high, Chels, and I am not paranoid, Chels, there's nothing to fear anymore for obvious reasons . . . But I am on fire, because I'm thinking of you and I know why you left me . . . It wasn't the fact I was married, but the fact I didn't see God's plan, which was that you and I were supposed to be. If I saw God in your face, then I have no faith in God, because I drove to Lino Lakes.

Holy Christ. I'm so high. This is different. There has to be a way to tone this down, because I am going to be sick in this place. I will likely keel over dead. This is terrible. I have to go for a walk. I need to get some air, and I can't even read what I'm writing, how could you? That's fine because you don't care. Please.

No, Chels. I love you. I love you. I always have forever even before I was born and I would never have left you and this whole thing might be different. I don't know anything, but my heart is going to explode, Chelsea.

Day Seven:
Transcript 3

I obviously survived.

Actually, it was good. It was a good feeling. At least when I came down a little. I really thought my heart was exploding at first . . . but . . . I did feel close to something authentic, high, touching the metal railings on bridges over the canals. Something real, sort of sublime, I guess, which I wanted.

I conflated God with drugs? Uh . . . I don't think so.

Don't you think there are drug users out there who are recreational users, who prefer smoking hash to—to—riding dune buggies—or fishing? Is every impractical act a search for God?

What are practical acts then?

Letter 23
September 18, 2004

Chels,

Cranberry left me a note while I was out high. We're supposed to go to Antwerp tomorrow, but he wants to take another day with Kaatje. Should I let him derail my plans? He did say, "Please." What about my truth finding? What about my search for the father I did not know? Should I let Cranberry go?

Yes. God bless him. I want him to find his Chelsea before it's too late.

Yes, his you. You've become my stand-in for great love. I mean, what if I met you now, on a plane headed for Amsterdam? What if I sat in the center aisle of a DC-10, between a mother with a screaming child and a girl with black hair and black eyes, who turned to me upon takeoff and said, "I dreamt about you last night"? What if we met now? I would throw everything else out, and we'd smoke hash together, maybe, or maybe we wouldn't need to, and we'd kiss on bridges and watch the bikers pass by, and we'd make love in a hotel. I'd give up everything for you now.

Okay. I'm breathing. Okay. I'm having a Coke (the soda).

Isn't it funny that I was reticent to be with you because I feared losing everything else and then I lost you along with everything else?

Why reticence? I had built a structure—a family, a house, a career. Even though the structure felt empty after a while, I built it. I owned it. It was something concrete to believe in. And even when my divorce was final last year, I didn't call you, because, I suppose, I hoped Mary would come back to me so I could reenter that structure, that home. I didn't have faith in God who I saw in you. I hedged. I was conservative. I was preservative. And I lost everything, including you, who made so much sense when nothing else did.

Go for it, Cranberry! Go for the GUSTO! Screw me, Cranberry, And Be With Kaatje!

I'm sorry I'm such a coward. I'm fighting sleep. I need more Coke.

T.

I got something right? What?

If you have faith, there is nothing to lose. Okay. So?

With God you are free because you know there's nothing anyone can take from you. You have God. They can even take your life, but they can't take away God, who is eternal, not destructible, right? So—so you're free to make courageous choices . . . like, what? To divorce your wife for another woman?

I think we're confused here. First, I don't think you can be courageous if every choice you have is easy. Second, I don't like your idea of faith. You don't have to have a nice bone in your body and you can be horrible . . . and arrogant . . .

I'm serious. Arrogance. There are World War II memorials all over Amsterdam.

Arrogance causes war, Father Barry. So many of these jerks think they've got God so they don't need to do anything else, because God is on their team. Dumbassed Americans think they can tear up the desert in their dune buggies . . . they can cheat on their taxes without fear, because they have God. Religious people are fantastic. God gives them an excuse to be brutal, and nothing

---

can touch them because they have God. Same logic underlies war, my man. You think Germans didn't have faith in their absolute? The Nazis had certainty, Barry. They knew they were right and God—whatever messed-up God they believed in—was with them, would reward them. Disgusting.

Secular? Not exactly, Barry. Power to the people! The *über* people. Big blond giant magical people! Pretty people who are free to kill because they believe in their divine right!

The Nazis had faith—maybe different rules and gods, but faith—just like you.

Did you just ask me to cool down?

Where are you going?

Oh shit, Chelsea.

Terrible.

The coffee shop where I had my several Cokes to stay awake apparently is only a moment's walk from the Red Light District. I just wanted to go back to the hotel, to have a beer, to calm down and watch a little Dutch TV before dinner. Instead, I was in the Red Light District after a short walk down the thinnest street ever—no cars could go there, only bikes, and the bikes nearly hit me, the street was so thin. And the windows, the many storefronts on this tiny street, as I walked apparently the opposite direction from the hotel, soon became filled with giant dildos of many colors, some more missile than penis. And right then, at the end of that street, the late day sun broke from behind the clouds, and although it is cool, moist, nippy, that darker sun in combination with the humidity, made me sweat, and the street, the next street after the thinnest street in the world, was filled with windows, and in the windows there were big-breasted African women in neon bikinis, beckoning with big dildos, waving dildos at me, puckering, rotating their hips and enormous, round asses, which made me sweat more. And the cold, sweaty heat was unbearable, so I pulled off my sweater as I walked, which brought the opening of doors, the whistling of women who wanted me to pay them for sex. So I hustled around the corner, which brought me to a street filled with Asian women in windows—apparently the marketplace is niche, segmented by race—who had smaller breasts and smaller asses and were wearing black or white bikinis and were not holding dildos but were posing as if in mid-orgasm, hips clenched then shaking, and were beckoning to me and to others. And outside some windows, groups of men stood making titty-pinching gestures and puckering-lip faces, and an American kid, a college kid, said to a teeny-tiny Asian girl who couldn't be more than twenty, "You can't handle this fat boy." And he grabbed his penis through his jeans, then to his friends, "Dude, my dick would totally destroy her." And then, prompted by his friends, high-fiving his friends, shouting, "Fuckin right," he entered the door next to the window with the tiny Asian girl and a curtain came down, so they were about to do it, whatever, right there behind a thin curtain as his boys stood outside that thin glass high-fiving, while this frat boy and his "fat boy" totally destroyed that poor girl. I know that can't be the case, but his intent—his intent. And I turned back, followed my streets back past Asians pressing their asses to glass and Africans pinching big pink missiles between their breasts, and then to the coffee shop where I last sat, where I last wrote you, where I am sitting now, dizzy, hot, not sure where my hotel is, without Cranberry, without you.

Day Seven:
Transcript 5

Maybe not. Maybe I didn't conflate sex and God or whatever, because I was really disturbed . . . I was heartbroken in the Red Light District.

Those young women and . . .

So animal. Like cattle. Living so other people can harvest your . . . Maybe I'm a prude.

No, not judgmental. Who am I to judge anybody? It just made me feel sad.

I did judge? Who?

Letter 25
September 18, 2004

Dear Mrs. Stemke,

You may not remember me. I was in your homeroom in seventh grade.

Listen. I had an obsession with your breasts, and so I couldn't concentrate on social studies. This was before my conscious understanding of sexual attraction. You wore very silky dresses. I could hear them husk over your bottom when you walked, which did something to me I didn't understand. Do you love your husband?

Listen. I broke into your garage when I was in seventh grade. Your husband had a lot of tires in there. Or maybe that was your tire pile. Who knows? All those silky dresses don't seem to match up to a lady who'd own a big pile of tires. Once in there, in your garage, I had no idea what to do—I think I wanted to play with your stockings. But you didn't have any stockings (or underpants or dresses) in your garage, just tires and cases of soda. I stole a case of Fresca from the corner, which I drank in my own garage until I got really ill. I just wanted to say I'm sorry for that.

Jesus. I'm in Amsterdam and I walked through the Red Light District accidentally a few moments ago, and now I know that non-completely-mutually desired sex is not nice, is horrible, as is sexual obsession. I feel so guilty about thinking about you the way I did and wanting to steal your stockings. I am so sorry.

Enclosed you'll find a twenty-dollar bill, which I hope will cover for the damages (Fresca-related and emotional).

T. Rimberg

Letter 26
September 18, 2004

Dear Madonna,

In 1986 you caused me to have an erection that lasted eight days. I thought I'd have to be hospitalized—it hurt me terribly.

You made your bazillions turning sixteen-year-old boys into sex addicts. You taught my classmates to dress like prostitutes, which only made my sex addiction worse. You're not the only one, of course. But you were the best, and your legacy is amazing. Look at the horrifying little pop singers you helped spawn. Their music is all about vibrating sex organs. I have twin nine-year-old daughters.

Just thought you should know I'm going to kill myself.

Sincerely,

T. Rimberg

Letter 27
September 19, just after 1 a.m. local

Hey Chels,

Shrooms taste terrible but okay with a Coke. I love Coke. What a product. It is a perfect refreshing drink, except for what cane worker in Haiti paid with his back for this sugar? It is delicious. But I can't help to think I'm drinking the blood of Haitians who die for Coca-Cola Co. I went to dinner with Kaatje and Cranberry, and Kaatje told me the Indonesians who served us food are victims of capitalist oppression. They make delicious food. Haitians who die for Coca-Cola? It is absurd. Everything must be built and there are designers and there are those who build and there are those whose function it is to extract the raw materials from the ground, and these laborers are paid for their labor, which provides them with a little spending money but not enough to buy a Coca-Cola, the most delicious drink in the universe.

You are not made impure by colonial oppression, capitalist logic. You are you, in the now and not trapped by history, like I am. Do you know why I'm here? My father. But you are sweet like Coca-Cola. Your blood is red like this little red label on this little glass bottle. Who makes these bottles? They are so beautiful and cool when pressed against my forehead. You are like sweet Coca-Cola and the cool feeling of this bottle on my forehead. I'm going to put you on my forehead again now. Now I am going to drink you from this bottle. I am so turned on I can hear bells ringing in my ears. There might be bells ringing? There are some church bells ringing. I'm going to go to church, Chels. I love you and I am drinking you.

Day Seven:
Transcript 6

So don't go thinking the Red Light District changed me in any fundamental way. Didn't stop me from getting all sexy about Chelsea, who was my girlfriend when I was married, did it?

No. I couldn't shut up. I was sort of manic.

Okay, very manic.

Read the next one. The shit hit the fan, Father Barry.

Chelsea,

I am thirty-five years old.

When we were together, I was thirty-three and almost thirty-four. Before we were together, I felt too old to go to a bar, thought it was wrong to go to a bar at thirty-three. There was no doubt about something else: I would never kiss another woman other than my wife. To do so would be wrong. I would go to the mall at lunch and have a coffee in the mall and look at women walking past, pushing strollers, talking on cell phones, and sometimes I would be attracted to them, and then I'd go home and help with dishes, and I would never kiss another woman. That is right and I wanted to be right. Do you think I would take drugs? I had it reined in, Chelsea.

I would not have taken drugs: no pot, no mushrooms.

I lived right but felt wrong. Never felt right. What is right?

It occurred to me, early this morning, while I was tripping on mushrooms: I think God hates me, because I've stopped obeying rules. And I think God loves me, because I've stopped obeying rules that keep me from killing myself, which is what I want to do. Then I think God hates me, because I stopped obeying rules completely only when I decided to kill myself. But then God must love me, because I love Chelsea and it wasn't about sex, it wasn't about physical gratification. I made a choice, used my free will not to buy a large truck or a speedboat or a freezer in which to store meats, not to go to strip clubs, which is wrong, but to kiss the woman I love completely. But I was not courageous enough to actually make a change in my life, so I didn't really make a choice, so God must hate me.

I heard bells. I understood the bells were ringing because of an incredible religious festival going on, even though it was late at night or early, early morning. I knew it was happening. There were people packing the streets in a reverie, and I knew something big and religious and important was going down. Light filled the sky, coloring the sky, twisting in the sky. The bells rang. Through the winding streets, in and out of alleys and between moving trams and speeding bicycles, I chased the sound of the bells. And I could tell I was getting closer, because the ringing became louder and louder, and people in the street moved to the rhythm of these ringing bells, were inspired by the bells, the big dance of life. And I walked and walked and walked and then got back to the bar where I started. Confused, and maybe desperate, I asked people where the bells were coming from, and most shoved me away, and some told me there were no bells, which I couldn't believe, because I could hear them ringing so clearly and then frantically, like they were warning of an air raid, but all the people told me no bells or get away and then I remembered: drugs. I am escaping reality. Not understanding. Escaping the earth to have a spiritual experience.

What if everything is made up, Chelsea? What if cities and governments and businesses and museums and bicycles are not perfect, not perfectible, not that Aristotelean perfect possibility, because there is no such thing as perfect, nothing God made, no God? What if everything is an accretion of human learning simply in existence because its function pleased someone like me, a completely flawed jerk?

What if there is no truth? No right path? What if everything is random?

Then I am no sinner, because there is no sin.

And if there is no sin, then the Nazis were not sinners. Hitler convinced a whole country to serve an ideology. A whole country became a murdering machine. But it was just a machine. It was just an invention like everything else. Not right or wrong. Chelsea, oh no. That can't be.

I'm lost. I'm here for my dad, not to take drugs. I'm alone. I'm here to find out what happened to my father. But what if it doesn't matter, Dad doesn't matter, because there is no God and everything is made up, there is no truth?

Chelsea. Please.

Letter 29
September 19, 2004

Dear Anne Frank,

I took a ride on a canal late this morning, here in Amsterdam. I was asleep for most of it, because I had a very difficult night, no thanks to me. (I took drugs and walked around like an idiot talking about the purity of pure love, which led me to stop believing in God.) I slept on that canal boat, with the lolling waves and the noise of the engine. But I woke up at the moment we passed your house, or at least the house where you hid until the Nazis came and hauled you away. Most of my family got hauled away, too. Maybe you knew them in Auschwitz. They were from Belgium. That's close to Holland. I'm not really Jewish (German mother—my family is culpable on that side).

Anne, Anne. I have daughters, and I would kill anyone who would harm them. I harm them.

Anne, Anne. I know that photo. I think it's a still from a film where you were looking out the window of your parents' apartment, tiny girl, looking down on the street at a wedding party, smiling, so beautiful. I wish you would've lived.

Anne, I went to an Indonesian restaurant before I took drugs. It's called Tempo Doeloe. The Indonesians are so nice. They smile and bring plate after plate filled with food. I wish you were in your seventies, elderly, eating in that restaurant, loving the beautiful service and the wonderful food.

But Anne, are the Indonesians victims, too? I've been told by Kaatje, whom you don't know, that they are victims. I suppose they are victims, if there is such a thing as a victim. Who isn't a victim? Me. I victimize, but not because I want to. Except I choose to, so maybe I want to. I am without intent to hurt my family, but I will and have hurt them. And the Indonesians bring wine, Anne. Not bad wine. Then I slept on the canal boat because I was on drugs last night. I'm sorry.

The Indonesians are in Holland because the Dutch invaded their country a long time ago. Dutch culture was perpetrated on them (if perpetration is possible, given that I'm not quite sure anything is real). And they cook very well but are displaced. I wish you had been displaced. I wish you had fled, a refugee. I wish you were an old lady in your adopted home, Queens, New York, an anonymous old lady, sweet and fat, living among Koreans and Russians, all displaced, but alive and maybe mostly happy. You were left behind and you died, a little brilliant girl, for no reason. I don't understand why these Indonesians are so happy to be serving food to the Dutch. Except they weren't left behind in the way you were. They are lucky.

Anne, I woke up at your house and I am empty and sad, and I miss my mother and my wife and my children and their excellent little friends who played in our backyard, like you should've played, and I'm here chasing my Jewish father who did not die in the war, when he might have, and I feel terrible guilt, like my father must have felt guilt for so many dead when he wasn't dead, and I miss my butler, who is not my son, and I miss being with my love, like you were with that boy Peter, remember that crush you had? I recognize that crush, your crush in the middle of the occupation, you told it so beautifully, so well, such a genius girl.

Anne. You mean a lot to me right now. You are proof there is beauty and right and wrong. What happened to you can't be anything but wrong.

I'm sorry, Anne.

Sincerely,

T. Rimberg

Day Seven:
Transcript 7

No more God.

Yes right and wrong . . . sort of. No more God.

I was changed, Barry. That night changed me. Writing Anne Frank changed me. Oh, but I was a changed man!

I'm not enjoying this today.

Okay. Before that stupid drug trip, I assumed—without thinking about it—there is "right" and "wrong" writ large, that there's an organizing principle that I don't make up. That exists. God's truth, or whatever. But what God? Not God! From humans! Learned!

I'm trying to explain.

Okay. My life was filled with regret for making "wrong" choices. Wrong implies the opposite, too: that there is a right.

Bingo. I figured that wrong and right is just a proxy for—you know—personally pleasant and unpleasant. And one man's pleasant is another's unpleasant.

Nazis find a world with no Jews pleasant. Jews don't agree. Because there were more Nazis in Germany than there were Jews, it became "truth" that the world would be better without Jews. That's not truth. That's a popularity contest that Jews lose big-time. But try telling the Nazis it isn't the truth. Nazis created the truth in Germany.

If there is no truth, there is no God, in the way I conceived God, and my actions don't matter—or at least . . . who should care about my actions? People should mind their own business. The damn truth is I was sort of religious or at least a believer. Before. I believed in big truths. But not after Amsterdam.

You're right . . . you're right . . . there was more to the change . . . from the Anne Frank letter. I took responsibility for making truth . . . I determined my own truth . . . through interacting with the world . . . because Anne was a person like me and I find people . . . most people to be decent and sweet . . . what happened to Anne was horrible . . . I was muddled. I'm tired, Barry.

Yes, it's in my journal. The little girl in my dreams reminded me of Anne Frank.

My whole demeanor changed after that. I stopped acting crazy.

I'm very tired.

Journal Entry, September 19, 2004

I don't need to go to Antwerp.

Antwerp, Belgium, because you think your father is there, because of stupid pictures of there. He is not there. He has already willed you money, because he is dead. Do you need to honor him by going? Do you need to figure out the truth? No. Remember when he came into your bedroom and woke you and whispered, "Theodore. I am not coming home again. This is not because of you." Remember hugging his neck and crying and the smell of aftershave, like he just shaved in the middle of the night? His neck and his aftershave. He smelled like your father. He was your father. He left you, which was wrong, because it hurt you, and you don't need to forgive him, and you don't need to find him.

Dear Chelsea,

This is it. I won't write to you again.

You could be with me. I'm not bound by marriage. It doesn't matter.

I'm leaving Amsterdam (and you).

This is goodbye.

T.

Day Seven:
Transcript 8

I went to Paris, yes. Why not?

Not okay. I'm sick.

CNN?

No. I don't want to be interviewed, Barry.

Thank you.

Journal Entry,
September 22, 2004, Still Amsterdam

This morning, you lay in bed, thinking that this would be the day. No overdosing—swim into the North Sea.

Last night again filled with war dreams, death dreams, fleeing families gunned down. Watched them like movies. No reaction. The same images played over and over. Kids dragging suitcases. Parents dragging kids. Old people stumbling and beaten. Then claps of sound, collapse, pools of blood. That's the way it is.

It's time to swim into the North Sea.

But then a call from the lobby.
Cranberry wants to meet for a beer. You say no.
Cranberry says Kaatje wants to speak. You say no.
Kaatje on the phone says her grandfather killed himself, but he had lung cancer and was surrounded by family.

They come to your room. They roll away your suitcase. And then the street and past people on feet and all those slow bikers and phallic symbols commemorating the war dead and then to the train.

This is not how you planned it. A high-speed train to Paris, flying past Antwerp. It's fine to say goodbye in Paris.

Day Eight:
Transcript 1

Guess what happened to me this morning! Wait. Are you recording already?

The letters on the train? I was saying goodbye.

I want to tell you what happened.

Okay. Read the letters to me.

Letter 31
September 23, 2004

Dear David,

    I'm on my way to Paris today. I've always been hard on you. I always thought you were not a nice person. Maybe you're not a nice person or maybe I never gave you a chance. I'm sorry regardless.

    T.

Letter 32
September 23, 2004

Dear Mary,

Paris was good to us in 1994. Remember the orange sky? That hot wind that blew your hair across my face? Your parents were sweet to take Charlie for the week. We were twenty-four years old and already had an eighteen-month-old kid. Amazing to have that joy and responsibility and terror so young.

Remember the lights on boats and bridges, the Seine? And we kissed up there, like a couple of star-struck Americans, which we were, ridiculous . . . except, the Eiffel Tower is all that. It is not a disappointment. It is beautiful, impossible, so authentic, even though it is a tourist trap. I loved being with you there on an orange Paris night. It is a powerful memory. You were pregnant with our girls.

So I'm going back to Paris today. First time since we were there together in our Salad Days. Our history after that trip ruined Paris. My behavior and your behavior, too . . . I think. That lovely 1994 Paris is gone for us. I'm sorry.

You are a good person, Mary. I know. You are a remarkable, beautiful, strong, good person.

T.

Dear Charlie, Kara, and Sylvie,

I am going to Paris and if I don't return, it will be because I fought the good fight. Imagine me, hunchbacked, wearing a burlap sack, ringing bells in Notre Dame, jumping from wooden beams, grabbing and swinging, riding the ropes up and down all over the immense tower. I will ring bells so they can be heard all over the city. The bells will sing: I love Charlie—Ding! I love Kara—Dong! I love Sylvie—Ding! But this pursuit is not without its risks and I may not make it out. Don't worry. Those bells will have the memory of my love for you vibrated into their metal. My love for you will live forever and ring out over all of Paris whenever those bells are rung. So wish me luck! This will be dangerous!

I love you all,

Dad

Day Eight:
Transcript 2

Oh, that's nice stuff. Thanks. Thank you for reading them.

Listen, Barry . . . I got really engaged talking yesterday. I really felt what I felt when I was in Amsterdam and I don't want to . . . Paris was horrible. I can't live it over again.

Thank you.

Don't you want to know what happened to me this morning?

You know?

I'd say attacked! It was unreal, Barry. I sat down on the couch to finally watch CNN. I heard a preview story as I was walking back from breakfast, so I thought I'd hang in the TV room to watch. Why not? And these poor sick people are all around, and when I sit, the old guy next to me grabs my arm and says, "I know who you are." He cranes his neck at me and shouts, "I know who you are." Then he folds over onto my lap and I scream for the nurse . . . I mean . . . I thought he was having a stroke. My other arm is in this cast. I couldn't pry him off me.

No. He's okay. No stroke. Just so weak he couldn't brace himself on his arm, and he went to sleep with his head in my lap.

Attacked again. I hate hospitals. So I didn't see any of my coverage on CNN. Still.

Every time I'm in one of these . . . institutions, I get attacked by the patients. Old people love to have at me, I guess.

I know. The recorder's on.

Yeah. Kaatje. She thought she was going to save me with self-help. She brought a book. Ridiculous, but kind of sweet, too. We stayed in this English hotel where one of her friends worked, so we got a good discount . . . and in the morning, Kaatje took out this book. I can't remember its name—*Play to Win*? And we're in the garden . . . in the middle of this beautiful Paris block, these vine-covered walls around us . . . fall with crisp air and sun . . . it was gorgeous back there. I actually remember thinking "pretty" but not having it affect me, just thought "pretty." I'd gone cold but knew it was gorgeous. And Kaatje pulled out this book about anxiety and depression and transcending all of that. It made no sense and I didn't listen. And she talked at me for maybe an hour. Kept flipping through pages, saying, "Listen to this. Here. You can retrain your thinking processes." Stuff like that. I felt like I was packed in cotton . . . or like my whole body was filled with cotton . . . like I was dried out and everything seemed apart from me, watching the world through the eyes of someone I didn't know and didn't care about.

It didn't go on very long. Kaatje got frustrated, real red in the face. And then, because I wasn't really listening, she said maybe I should go to a hospital, and Cranberry nodded, sort of nervously, but he agreed I should go to a hospital. Then I told them I felt a little dizzy and needed to go get a drink of water.

I didn't come back for several days.

I walked, let my mind wander. It was strange to have my memories and thoughts but to feel so separate from them. There was nothing desperate about how I experienced this. I didn't intend to return to the hotel.

At times . . . sometimes I would sit at a bar or a café and write a little. I carried that backpack everywhere. I sat under a bridge next to the Seine and wrote, too. Mostly I just watched.

I wrote to Bill Clinton. But I wrote other stuff, too.

Journal Entry,
September 25, 2004, under a bridge next to
the Seine

What's a pogrom? Remember it means "devastation" in Russian. But is it a slaughter or just a riot? Anti-Jew. Pogrom burned the houses down. Burned down the synagogue. When I close my eyes, I see the fires. Not sure if I'm fleeing or if I'm the one who set them.

Journal Entry,
September 25–26, 2004, under a bridge next to the Seine

Dream: Across the street there is the park where kids ride their bikes. They shouldn't be riding in that park. What if someone takes them? You can feel the ground shaking. Those are tanks rolling on cobblestone. Those are gas lamps quivering. You pull a chair to the window, but can't sit down, because you realize you're carrying the girl piggyback style, although she is too old to be carried. So you stand and watch the children riding bikes at twilight while the gas lamps shake. A voice from a bullhorn is shouting. People start pouring from doors all around the neighborhood. They're dragging suitcases and pillows and they're dressed in coats, although it's summer and the trees have leaves and it seems warm. Bullhorn is so loud, telling them all to gather. You turn to your right. Is it your father shouting? Is it you watching your father? The little girl on your back holds your ears. The people get on trains.

Letter 34
September 26, 2004

Dear President Clinton,

My wife was pregnant in the summer of 1992. She was just my girlfriend then. We were both twenty-two and I was trying to finish college. There was another girl in my cultural anthropology class that summer who had the thickest, most beautiful hair I've ever seen. It was thick ropes of dark red. She wore patchouli oil and white hippie dresses that danced around her hips when she walked into class. She had a wide tanned face and thick dark lips and green eyes. Her beauty made no sense. She was amazing.

My girlfriend lay pregnant in our studio apartment sweating, her stomach swelling, her breasts swelling, my son growing inside of her, and there I am in my cultural anthropology class losing my mind over this girl. It didn't occur to me to feel guilty.

But one day the patchouli girl came in late. She came in during a lecture on the phallus-driven rituals of the Balinese cockfight. She squeezed past me in the row, her skirt brushing my legs, her patchouli expanding around me. She sat down next to me, and I breathed her. Then she leaned over and asked me if we could meet after class so she could look at the notes she'd missed. I melted. I would kiss her. I would touch her shoulders and her face. I would lie down with her. And then I remembered my girlfriend pregnant on our futon, and for a moment I became enraged that I had been trapped by this girlfriend and this horrible thing inside her. And then such an intense guilt washed over me, such a sadness, I got sick. I stood, told Professor Lewis I was sick, and stumbled out of the room.

For the first time, the enormity of the situation—I had procreated, I had made a life, I was not a good person—sank in. I stumbled away from class, down Bascom Hill, and because I could not go to my apartment to face my girlfriend, I went to the library, and after hyperventilating and slapping water on my face, and throwing up a little in the bathroom, I picked up a magazine, *The Atlantic Monthly,* to try to take my mind off things.

That magazine contained a great interview with you, then Governor Clinton, candidate Clinton. You talked about integrity in that article. You said you were obsessed with the word *integrity*. Integrity, literally integrating mind, body, and spirit, so that one is ready for any challenge, so that one naturally acts on deep convictions. I was so moved, I trembled.

Here was an answer, maybe. I thought about Balinese cockfighting, beautiful girls on Bascom Hill, the girl in class with her ropes of red hair, and Mary, my girlfriend, pregnant on our futon. Integrity, I thought, could save me.

Starting that day, I had a burst of positive energy like I'd never had before. I stood up tall and made lists of my values, made lists describing the kind of father I wanted to be. I quit smoking. I started running. I quit my job at the deli in the student union (where night after night I'd stolen beer and gotten drunk) and applied for a job canvassing, going door to door fundraising for the environment, fundraising to save Wisconsin's wetlands. I got the job. I even started meditating to discipline my mind.

President Clinton, by my twenty-third birthday in August, I felt in control. I felt powerful. I knew who I was and what I wanted. I had integrity.

But there was a problem. A values problem. What I believed in was not the values themselves but the feel of having integrity, a feeling of power. I liked looking good to others (my mother, my girlfriend's parents). Sure, I wrote on my lists that honesty, kindness, generosity, action, etc., were my values. What does all that mean? Yes, I said I wanted to save the environment (fashionable convictions in Madison, Wisconsin), but I wasn't a true believer. Environmentalism won me friends. If people liked me, that was a sure sign that I was in the right, a good person.

This is a flawed premise, and it led to trouble.

Two weeks before your election I was training a new canvasser named Hannah Garrity. We canvassed a college house filled with drunk guys who said they'd give money if we had drinks with them. We had drinks. We talked environmental issues passionately, even though the drunk guys couldn't have cared less. Hannah was amazed by me, by my power, my abilities. She was tall and skinny, and we were completely naked and ready to have sex before I thought about what I was doing and ran away, ran home to my sleeping girlfriend, she so pregnant. I cried next to her and she said, "It's okay . . . It's okay . . . these are hard times." I bawled.

Earlier in the fall my girlfriend told me she'd like to kill me and if she had a gun she would gladly put a bullet between my eyes. Hormones are crazy, and we didn't have any chairs in our apartment so she had to lie there all day long. I knew things were rough and I had integrity, I believed, and told her then, at that moment she said she'd like to kill me, "Everything will be okay. I will take care of you forever." She broke down sobbing, and I hugged her and kissed her wet cheeks.

My son, Charlie, was born on the day you were elected. I wanted to name him William Jefferson Clinton Rimberg. Thankfully, Mary said no.

Mary divorced me later.

I'm in Paris. I walked almost all day yesterday and saw plenty of students, which reminded me of you and integrity.

Integrity is dangerous. Literally integrating mind, body, and spirit? What spirit? I think we made up spirit to hide from the fact of our animalness. Integrity feels good, because it limits uncertainty. It gives you easy answers. But integrity stems from popular values, not from the spirit (which is made up).

Think of it.

Values come from mass culture. What if you grew up watching gyrating women in music videos and you've learned to value sex? Wouldn't integrity demand you have a lot of sex? What if you were born into a value system that detests Jews? Wouldn't killing Jews be a fully integrated action? What if popularity is the most important thing in your society? Wouldn't an integrated person do whatever it takes to be popular? Integrity means what, President Clinton? That you act on your values? What if the only values out there are shit?

I know this is a simplification, but it bothers me. I think most behavior is mob behavior, even when it doesn't look like it. I'm not a fan of mobs. I'm not a fan of this place. I'm not a fan of yours, although I used to be. I'm sorry.

I guess this is another suicide letter.

T. Rimberg

Letter 35
September 26, 2004

Dear Uncle Jim (or the Owner of Uncle Jim's Pizza), Madison,
Wisconsin,

Hello. I'm very tired. I slept under a bridge in Paris next to
the Seine, just for a couple of hours, I'm sure. I'm not going to be
alive much longer, but had to write this. This is my last apology.

In October of 1992 I'd thought I'd found my calling. I went
door to door for WISPIRG, the Wisconsin Public Interest
Research Group, raising money to save the wetlands. Although
I'd struggled to raise a cent in Rush Limbaugh suburbs, where
they called me a tree hugger and feminazi, I'd learned I could talk
college students into giving up a portion of their beer money very
easily. I set records for the organization in student neighborhoods,
and I became terribly arrogant about my abilities.

I believed that I knew what I believed in: saving the wetlands.
And I thought, the ends justify the means. Saving the wetlands
might mean I'd have to talk about music with punks or Vespas
with Mods or football with jocks or counterpoint in Bach with
geeky cello players or vandalism with vandals or my hatred of FIBs
(fucking Illinois bastards) with rednecks from northern Wisconsin.
I really loved talking rednecks into giving money for the
environment. I could lie and say FIBs were destroying Wisconsin
floodplains with their summer homes. I could also say that hunters
helped the environment by facilitating the circle of life.

As long as I raised money, I'd tell the students whatever they
wanted to hear. The fact is, I didn't believe in saving the wetlands.
I believed in being loved, being a superstar, winning. I believed in
believing in something and making it happen. Integrity.

One night I went to a house full of rednecks to ask them to
donate money. I talked a lot about FIBs and hunting and

snowmobiles with them. They loved me and said they'd put out the money, but only if I came back later to drink at their keg party.

I was training another canvasser that night by the name of Hannah Garrity. She was from Chicago but didn't seem to mind me calling a FIB a FIB. She told me, after having two beers at the rednecks' apartment, that I reminded her of Bill Clinton, because I could talk to all kinds of people about what mattered to them. Three houses later, we took shots of vodka to get some Mod kids to contribute money. They gave us $35. Outside that house, I told Hannah Garrity about how I had integrity, and then I kissed her. Power is sexy and I was drunk. She didn't know my soon-to-be-wife Mary was back in my apartment wondering if her Braxton Hicks contractions were real contractions.

By nine, at the end of the shift, Hannah and I were really drunk and we both thought it'd be fine to keep the money we'd raised in my bag overnight, and we walked toward the redneck kegger arm in arm.

The party was filled with sweatshirted Wisconsin boys and girls. They stared at us when we walked in, but the guys we talked to before were happy to see us, especially one guy, a huge one, who loved to bow hunt. His name was Tim. He jumped off the couch when we came in and hugged us both, screaming, "You showed up . . . I love you fuckers," and we became part of the crew. And the place wasn't filled with Republicans, like I figured it would be. A whole bunch of them said they were voting for Bill Clinton. "You damn right you are," I told them, high-fiving each one. Then somebody put on AC/DC and we passed a one-hitter around and around and around, and when I got up to go to the bathroom, Hannah Garrity followed me.

Inside the bathroom she said, "I want to bite your neck and your ears."

I smiled.

And we took turns peeing in that bathroom, as if it were obvious we should do so. This ridiculous free peeing might have signaled to me that something wasn't working properly, and I should go home, should call it a night and go home to pregnant Mary, but it seemed right; it felt so good. I felt perfect, loved, integrated, and I stumbled against the hall walls walking back to the living room, ecstatic to be with people who adored me.

Somebody called out for cash so they could go buy tequila.

I pulled ten twenties out of my canvassing bag and handed it to the tequila buyer and said, "Get ten bottles."

The party whooped and clapped. I was a star.

Then a loud conversation started. FIBs again. People were pissed about FIBs. "They drive like idiots," someone shouted. "My dad can't afford the taxes on our cabin because FIBs drive up the property values," said another. "They're cutting down Wisconsin forests to build their stupid summer homes," I shouted. "We're losing our goddamn songbird habitat." And then everybody got so angry, especially after someone mentioned the Chicago Bears.

And then I had an idea. It seemed important. Praxis. Do you know what Praxis is, Uncle Jim? Bill Clinton talked about it in an interview I read in 1992. It means putting knowledge and beliefs to work. *Acting* on your beliefs.

"You know what?" I said. "I've been walking around in this neighborhood all day, and there are huge amounts of FIBs. Check out the license plates. We should get the fuck rid of those ugly-ass license plates. Show some respect . . ."

Everyone shouted, "Goddamn right we should." And the whole crew, girls and boys and Hannah Garrity, too—even though, as I mentioned, she was from Chicago—stumbled down the dark stairs of the apartment and spread out across downtown to get rid of license plates from the State of Illinois. Praxis. Beliefs into action.

Me, Hannah, and Tim took off together. And the FIB plates were everywhere we looked. We ripped FIB plates off Toyotas and Pontiacs and Hondas and BMWs (which had honking alarms) and a Volkswagen Cabriolet, whose whole bumper came off when big Tim yanked on the plate, and we almost died laughing, falling over, high-fiving. And then Tim started hurling license plates, and they'd curl and they'd bend in the air beautifully, loop-to-looping, catching the light of the streetlights above, crashing against houses, causing people to shout out from their windows, "I'm calling the cops." And I threw a plate that boomeranged around and almost hit Hannah in the face, except I knocked it out of the air in front of her. "I love you," Hannah told me. "I love you, too," I said back, and we stood there and kissed.

By then we were across West Washington Avenue, and Tim was convinced that Uncle Jim's Pizza, your pizza place, Uncle Jim, was a FIB establishment, and so we kicked in your windows and threw FIB license plates through the broken glass. I took an immense amount of joy in doing so.

Then we heard cop sirens and spread out and ran, losing each other. Hannah and I met up again in back of a nearby apartment building. We made out, then walked to Hannah's apartment four blocks away and stumbled up the stairs. We took off each other's clothes, stifling laughter, and fell onto her futon, but then Hannah began to cough and needed a drink of water, and she turned on the lights and I saw that her futon cover was the same India print futon cover I'd purchased with my pregnant girlfriend Mary two months before.

And as Hannah walked out of the room, naked, I remembered Mary and my baby and the money at the redneck house spent on tequila and Mary and my baby and Bill Clinton and the wetlands and FIB plates flying through the air . . . and my Mary . . . and my Mary . . . and I fell onto the floor trying to get my pants on, crying about all the poor babies, me as a baby, me without my father, and my poor baby, and all that broken glass and your face, Uncle Jim, your sad face, and my Mary, my Mary.

"What are you doing, man?" Hannah asked, standing in the doorway, so skinny and naked, two glasses of water in her hands, as I pulled on my clothes.

"I don't know . . . I don't know . . ." And I left.

And I ran all the way home, so afraid Mary would be gone, at the hospital, having our baby alone. But she was there, asleep on our futon, and I fell onto her sobbing.

As I said, I'm in Paris, Uncle Jim. I hung around the Sorbonne yesterday. Walked, sat at a café. The students don't look like Wisconsinites or FIBs or rednecks, but I'm sure they're capable of the crimes I committed. They want to be somebody. They want to be loved and respected. They want to feel right. They'd smash your windows. They'd dress like soldiers and shoot us all, if given the right context. They'd do it to feel good and right. To be a part of the team. They're just like you and me, Uncle Jim.

I don't want to be like them or me or you. I will be done and I want you to know how sorry I am that I did what I did. I am so sorry.

T. Rimberg

Journal Entry,
September 27, 2 a.m., under a bridge next to the Seine

Just woke up. Just dreamed this:

You are walking with kids on either side. Charlie is on the right, Kara and Sylvie on the left. We're in a hall in a large basement, low lights, bare bulbs and the earth is shaking around us. We're moving fast. The heat is rising in your face. We turn left at a T in the hall and down another. Machine-gun fire sounds, sporadic—like they're aiming and firing, not spraying—from upstairs. The kids are breathing so hard, louder than our footsteps. Shh, you say. But Kara is gulping air. She is going to cry. She says, Daddy. We go through a door into a dark room. You feel the walls around the door for a light switch. Can't find a switch. You reach into the air, grasping for a pull cord. Your kids are whimpering. You find a cord, machine-gun fire closer, maybe in the stairwell you just passed. You pull the cord. Light explodes. And Dad is smiling in the middle of the room. Corpses in striped camp uniforms are piled all around him, with eyeglasses, gold teeth, suitcases. Dad is not dead. He shakes his head, raises his eyebrows, extends his arms, says, "It is too late. Lights out." And then blackness.

That's it. You are not going to have another dream.

Journal Entry,
September 27, under a bridge next to the
Seine

Fully clothed. Pockets stuffed with broken concrete. I'm in.
Blow out air. Say goodbye. Goodbye. And sink. Down. Down.
Surrounded by dark cold, cold and green, cold and blue, and
bubbling up. Up? Big lights. Streetlights. Air and light and
bridge. Blow out again. Go limp, go still. Goodbye Charlie.
Goodbye Mary. Goodbye. Sink through green to blue. Let go.
And darkness. And bubbles. And up. Blue. Green. Up. Bubbling
up. Exploding light and bubbling up. The bridge. The city. The
surface. Then suck. Breathe water in. Drink water. Drink dirty
water. Drink it. And down. Cough. Coughing water out. Lights
everywhere, big bubbles of light on top of the water and the
current should be carrying you away. It's not.

On the bank. Angry. Hit head on wall. Awake.

In. Bleed from head. Shark bait. Blow out. Blow air. Suck water.
Fill lungs. Sink. Light light light, bubbles, back up. No sharks
to take you. On the bank. Throw up this water, sick water, Paris
water. Vomit hard. Back in. Sink. Sink. Sink. Swallow. Eyes
burning, acid water. Sink. Can't sink. Please please. No. Back up.
Vomit. Bleed. In. No! No! No!

People shout from the bridge. You run away across Paris.

Day Eight:
Transcript 3

I wrote that an hour after my last attempt, sitting on the curb right before I barged back into the hotel to Kaatje and Cranberry, who had called to report me as a missing person.

Yes. Before this drowning farce I was thinking very clearly. I wasn't having romantic thoughts or heroic thoughts . . . I was killing myself rationally.

I couldn't stay under. I don't know. I just remember being pushed up every time. Maybe it was the bubbles?

When I got out of the river the final time, people were shouting at me from the bridge, wanting to help me—it was morning rush hour by then, so there were lots of people—and I shouted back at them, I screamed at them. I must have looked crazy. Then a policeman showed up on the bridge, and I grabbed my backpack and ran away.

I kept running through crowds and traffic . . . I was electrified, like shock treatment? Actually, I have no idea what that feels like.

I blame the Seine for my lungs now. I still can't stop coughing. I haven't recovered. Disgusting water. You can't imagine what I saw in that water.

No, the river couldn't kill me. I really tried.

It would've been a more definitive attempt if I'd jumped off the Eiffel Tower or off the top of Notre Dame. If I bounced, we'd know a little more, wouldn't we?

An hour after I got back to the hotel we were on a train north.

Why? Antwerp, Barry. Antwerp is north.

Journal Entry,
September 27, on damn train

Fell asleep for five damn minutes. But still in those five minutes you're right up there in the apartment with Dad and with little spooky dream sister, watching troops march. Dad turns and smiles. He says, "You do what you do to survive. Are you sorry to survive? Not a choice! The only option. Correct? Am I correct? And if you only have one choice, how can you feel sorry to make it?"

Shut up, Dad. Shut up! Shut up!

Day Nine:
Transcript 1

I slept hard last night. I didn't cough at all. Relieved to get past Paris, I guess.

Kaatje dropped us off in Antwerp on her way to Amsterdam. She had to go back to quit her job. She was back with us in Antwerp within a day.

I told her to do whatever felt right. When she said she was going to quit, I offered her up a high-five and said something like, "Slap me some skin, sister."

She did sort of high-five me. The Dutch aren't great at high-fives.

Not exuberant, no. Not drowning made me . . . maybe I was kind of exuberant? Energetic. But different than before . . . not like the zippy dipshit philosophical loser in Amsterdam.

Not concerned with the abstract, with ideas or whatever. I was driven to find out what the hell was going on. I wanted to understand what actually happened to Dad and to me, so I was focused.

We hit Belgium on the train, and I was like a dog, nose pressed against glass . . . I knew that flat countryside. From Julia

Hilfgott, sort of, when I'd traveled with her . . . but that wasn't it. I just know the Belgian countryside. My father lived in it.

When we got to Antwerp, I ran out of the train and ran straight from the train station all the way into the middle of the old city, where the cathedral is.

No map. I'd been there with Julia Hilfgott. Maybe that's why I knew where to run. It could also be that I was running directly away from a convoy of Nazi trucks that I saw parked at the station when I left the train. The Nazis were frightening to me, so I ran and was lucky enough to run into a pretty part of town. That's possible, too.

Yes. Broad daylight, 2004. I saw a convoy of Nazi trucks parked at the train station.

Yes, Barry, I would call that a vision. Or perhaps a hallucination.

It wasn't that far a run. Cranberry had it worse. I had run off the train with only my backpack. He had to roll both our suitcases and keep up with my running, while shouting at me, which couldn't have been easy.

I got us a hotel near the cathedral. From there I walked around for several days, searching, peering into the eyes of the enemy. Nazis everywhere, like from my dreams, except I was awake.

Letter 36
October 3, 2004

Dear Professor Lewis,

Waffles, Professor! Do you know there are waffles in Belgium? It's true. Belgian waffles. Do you remember when you taught my Survey of Ethnography class and talked about the phallic-driven rituals of the Balinese cockfight? That left a lasting impression on me. Preening, fluffing, all that cock violence. Your class made me so curious and made me feel so human, and you, Professor, turned me on to learning (although I've done nothing with my life until now).

I'm engaged in an investigation, Professor. My father is hidden from me! The nature of reality, the truth, it is all hidden. I hope you remember me. T. Rimberg? Scholar of human behavior and history?

I am sitting on a square in downtown Antwerp, Belgium. I've been coming back here again and again in the several days and nights I've been in town in order to observe and take notes. Have you been to Antwerp? I believe your area of expertise was Micronesia. Micro means tiny.

Antwerp (Antwerpen in Flemish) means "hand-throwing," literally "hand-throwing." I read that on a brochure about the city I found sitting on a table in this waffle restaurant. No, not hand-throwing as in throwing a pot with one's hands on a potter's wheel. Oh no! There's no making in this story. This throwing is about destruction.

Antwerpen. Hand-throwing.

Folklorically speaking, a young boy hero killed a bad giant a long time ago, cut off his hands, and threw them in the river right where modern Antwerp is. Thus the name Antwerp. Hand-throwing. This is meaningful to me. I threw myself in a river last week. In Paris. If this city were named for my throwing incident, it would be called "Rimbergwerpen" or "T.werpen." Funny, but true. As a scholar, I take knowledge gained and apply it to new situations to see how it fits. It fits good, Professor. I like "Rimbergwerpen" (literally Rimberg-throwing).

Check this out: I rose up from the river into which I threw myself. I know. But believe it. (Rimbergopklimmen—literally "Rimberg rising"—if I understood what the waffle waitress told me when I asked.)

Waffles.

So I'm sitting in the square, and there is an enormous, delicate cathedral nearby, hovering above everything—I am looking at its clock tower now. Yes, I remember it from when I was here in college (crazy trip). But it is bigger than I remember, which is amazing. Everything else I remember from when I was a youngster is diminished in size from memory. All my memories of big yards and big houses and big adults . . . when I see them again they are small and unimpressive. (I'd likely think you tiny if I saw you now.) But this cathedral is enormous.

Do you know what else is enormous in Antwerpen? Waffles!

They are much bigger than Eggo waffles. Me and my brother David (bastard) ate those sometimes when we were kids.

My dad hit David because of a waffle. One morning David and I were joke-fighting over an Eggo waffle (not real fighting, which was normally the case). A waffle popped out of the toaster, and we both grabbed for it, and we shouted back and forth, just like on the TV ad, "Leggo my Eggo!" My mom sort of laughed, rolled her eyes, and kept scurrying around the kitchen, putting our school lunches together. And the radio was on, local news, cattle prices. And it was warm and good in that kitchen. And me and David got louder and louder, shouting, actually having a good time with one another.

And then my father stormed in, grabbed the Eggo out of our

hands, tore it, and threw it in the garbage. He spat, "Fighting over cardboard shit." He slapped David on the ear, and he would've hit me, but Mom grabbed his arm. Father shoved her away and left the house.

Now I know why, Professor. The waffles in Belgium are magnificent. These waffles are worth fighting for. These waffles are the real thing. My dad must've eaten this kind of waffle growing up. Of course he was upset with us.

In order to understand human behavior, one must understand root causes, eh, Professor? Had I known about these Belgian waffles, I would've known a thing or two about my old dad.

Speaking of Dad, I'm quite sure I see Nazis walking around here. Not neo-Nazis, Professor. Old-fashioned, straight-out-of-the-movies-Nazis. It's confounding. This is my life's work, I think. This is what I'm here to do.

You've been a real inspiration to me.

Thank you,

T. Rimberg

Dear Aunt Jemima,

I'm sorry to say that you've been replaced in my heart by fresh fruit. The lord giveth and the lord taketh away. I only say this because I know from listening to NPR one morning a few years ago that you are named after one of the biblical Job's daughters. Poor, poor misused Aunt Jemima.

Job was Jewish.

I am real and I see Nazis and I'm in a city that was decimated by Nazis and my dad was born here and he was a Jew. That's bad. So don't complain! You're a racist trademark with a hanky on your head. Still I always loved you and your friend Mrs. Butterworth even though you are not real.

Don't complain to me! Especially now that I know a waffle should be covered in fresh fruit and whipped cream, not fake maple butter syrup, which I loved to pour on my Eggo waffles as a small child. I remember staring at your face on the syrup bottle, you smiling at me, while my brother screamed and cried and my mother screamed and cried and my dad slammed the door and left the house.

Sweet liquid and bad memories, Aunt Jemima, daughter of Job. I am in Antwerp, and we shall receive the good hand of the lord (and cut it off and throw it in the river?) and we shall receive evil, Aunty.

Thank you for being a friend.

T. Rimberg

Dear Professor Lewis, teacher of the phallic Balinese Cockfight,

More investigatory notes:

Antwerp is filled to the gills with Jews. I didn't remember this from being here with Julia Hilfgott. These Jews are present-day Jews, too, not just Jews from wartime who I dream when I'm awake. The city is filled with actual Jews. The only Jews I remember from my time here with Julia Hilfgott were her family members, who paid no attention to me, who made me feel not at home, which fueled my pain and anguish over leaving Molly Fitzpatrick in Dublin, which caused me to look at the ground and not at the beautifully Semitic Julia Hilfgott, even when Julia pleaded with me to be with her, because, she knew it, we belonged together. Oh, did Julia get upset!

Everybody's always so upset with me, Professor Lewis. Should probably take a hint, huh? I'm an upsetting person.

Other than the shit that was an inch from my own nose when I was here, I don't remember much of Antwerp.

Now I see everything.

I am an examiner, an investigator. I am tracking down my father, Professor, tracking, although that's a ludicrous inclination. I have every evidence he is dead. Still, here I am. I should be dead, too, but I'm not, I don't think, so that's something.

Professor, this morning, after several days of wandering and eating, I told the concierge at the hotel that I was looking to see Jewish stuff. I bet that's part of your investigatory process. Ask a local for info, someone in the know?

The concierge said, "The Shtetl? Diamond district? It is all very close."

"Shtetl?"

"Yes, Shtetl. I don't call it Shtetl. American tourists often, though. Shtetl because so many look in this neighborhood as if they are from a different century, in Poland maybe?"

"You mean all those Jews in hats aren't ghosts?" I shouted.

The concierge looked at me and didn't crack a smile. She looked mad, maybe, or concerned or annoyed, but she gave me a map. The one direction I haven't walked in this city leads directly to the Shtetl! The fact is every time I've started walking in that direction, I've seen Jews in hats whom I thought were ghosts and I've gotten terrified and run home. But they're alive!

Me, Kaatje, and Cranberry (long story—two young people with me—my research assistants, if you will) walked from our hotel toward this Shtetl. It's good little Kaatje and Cranberry came with me. I am cautious around them, because I know they are agonizing over my behavior (another long story, Professor) and have heard them discuss putting me in a hospital, which is not a good idea. With my research assistants around, I do not say what's on my mind, because I need to stay undercover in society. I can't scream when I see the Gestapo, because nobody but me is privy to their presence, and it's better for me not to set off alarm bells. Got it? To put it in terms an anthropologist would understand, I need to observe, not participate.

Sooo, get this. Not too far from our hotel, maybe a mile or so, we came to the Central Station. (Our train arrived at this station on the way into town, but I saw something strange and ran away from it without ever looking at it.) And, this station. With me finally really engaged in seeing it, really looking, I saw some stuff. I saw people in fur coats and children in hats and Stars of David and I saw bombs falling from the sky. Oh, I knew what was happening, and I was not pleased to know any of this. I knew something about this station. And not just because I see into the past, although that doesn't hurt.

In August, I received a package that contained several pictures of my likely dead father in front of this very station, standing with various formally dressed people—I assume family members or business associates? And there is a zoo next to this station, through this ornate, pretty gate. And also in the package there was a picture of my dead dad at ten years old or so, black and white, a beautiful little-boy Dad, looking like my son Charlie, standing at the gate of this zoo. The exact same gate I see now! My father is ten, but his face is morose. And I see this gate today, and I also see people in overcoats with Stars of David and men with military jackets blowing whistles, and also present-day businessmen. Whoa! My eyes! I cannot participate.

Me and my research assistants crossed the front of the domed station. In present day, the civic square in front of it is dug up for some kind of construction, so it isn't pretty, but the building, Professor, it is perhaps one of the most beautiful train stations anywhere, ever. Golden and darkening metal and dirty stone, but majestic. It scares the shit out of me.

Running along the right side of the station is a long street. This street is filled with diamond shops. As soon as we turned on this street, I knew we were getting close, close, close. Men with dark beards and dark hats rode bicycles. They did not wear Stars of David—these were present-day Jews. Hasidic Jews, so it's hard to tell they're from today. They wore dark wool coats, though the sun was shining and it was in the high sixties. Some were stopped together, in little droves of bicycles, speaking quietly to one another. There were also people who looked more like my dad, big men with big glasses and big rings, climbing out of expensive cars. These, I think, are modern Jews. There were also Indians—from India! Walking around! What do you make of that? Global economy. But mostly Jews.

Jews, everywhere. Some from the olden days, but mostly from right now, today. My dad once told me that only a few hundred

Jews were left in Antwerp after the war. I remember him saying it was terrible, terrible. And his parents dead . . . And his brother escaped to New York (where my dad would eventually follow). There have to be thousands of Jews in the city now. The diamond street was filled with them.

Because my research assistants were with me and I needed to mind my manners so they didn't commit me, I did not approach anyone on the street to get the lowdown, whatever that might have been.

Diamonds. I do believe my family dealt in diamonds, Professor, or still does.

Me and my assistants took a right from the diamond street into a little winding neighborhood where all the storefronts— clothes, grocery, pharmacy, bakery—were Jewish and had signs in Hebrew and, I assume, Yiddish. (That's what Kaatje thought—she is a Dutch speaker and her Dutch helps her even with Yiddish—I had no idea—language!) Mothers in dark coats pushed crying babies in strollers, with little boys bounding next to them in yarmulkes. The mothers' heads were covered in scarves or in obvious wigs. These are fundamentalists, Professor Lewis. They're like the Amish but with money and cars. And bicyclists in black hats and old rabbis with long gray beards and gray, grave faces and grave gaits, moving along with their hands clenched behind their backs. They all mumble. Everyone mumbles, mutters: men, women, children. Either to each other, or if alone, to themselves. I remember this from Dad. Their voices are always rumbling soft in their throats. I can hear it now. Just like my dad.

In a bakery, case after white case filled with beautiful foods, everything like something I know, but not exactly—cake-like, bread-like, pretzel-like—I caught fire, and even though my research assistants were with me, I stopped simply observing and began participating. I struck up a conversation in English with a middle-aged woman at the counter. Goose pimples raised on my skin. I told her my father lived in Antwerp before the war. And I ordered a knish and potato latkes, and she said, yes, and wrapped up my purchases, and yes, she lives around the block with her husband, who owns this shop, and yes, three children, and yes, blessings, all are doing well in school.

"Jewish school?" I asked.

She squinted her eyes at me, nodded.

So I nodded, paused, almost said a lot more, but didn't, because I wanted her to ask, wanted her to ask me my name, show she recognized me, but she didn't ask.

Then another woman entered the store, and the shop lady turned her attention to the woman, gravel talking, fast talking, nervous talking in Yiddish, and so I nodded and squinted at both of them, my eyes watering, and then my research assistants grabbed me by the arm and pulled me out of the store. I had my knishes, etc., so okay, fine.

Outside Kaatje said, "You should be careful. I think the shopkeeper was saying something not nice about you to that woman."

I'm getting closer in my investigation, Professor, closer to my father. I must tread delicately so as not to blow my cover. Yes. Careful I shall be! Fly under the radar. Not raise the eyebrows. I've got to keep my secrets.

We wandered awhile longer, the sun so warm in this place though I've been told it's cold, cloudy, and rainy here this time of year. We found a nicely landscaped park, with little hills, large hardwood trees, and long ponds. The park felt familiar, perhaps from my dreams, which I take seriously these days, even though social scientists like us perhaps should not. I saw kids pulling wagons and riding bikes, kids in 1940s woolen sweaters and khaki shorts, and I then considered my need for stealth, so looked away. The sun shone down, and there we sat and ate, Jews and Indians and Belgians all around. And without the earth shaking or the light changing, I saw jeeps pulling guns, panzers that disappeared into air, flashes of fires and marches of civilians, kids knocked to the ground, bleeding, and I couldn't react, so I looked to the sky, but there prop airplanes streaked, popping clouds and exploding, and so I shut my eyes.

Bakery shop. She knows me in the bakery shop, Professor. I know she recognized me. Perhaps she could provide me information as to the whereabouts of one Josef Rimberg, my father, who likely is or isn't deceased. (What's the difference?)

I will go about these inquiries with great stealth and control.

I wish you were here to guide me in my information gathering, Professor. You would be helpful and dispassionate and rational, unlike my research assistants, who watch me like hawks.

Yes, my father did hit David. I still wanted to find him. I wasn't angry at him for hitting David.

I don't think Dad hit me, but I do remember him trying that one time.

No way I would've contacted David. He's my brother only by blood.

Right, I felt closer to this Professor Lewis, who taught all of these incredible ethnographies that included magic and a lot of violence and scientific discovery. It made more sense to contact him . . . write to him. You know what I mean.

I don't really know Professor Lewis. I don't even know if he's alive anymore. But I needed to write someone who might understand.

God, yes. I can still see it, Barry, both dream and reality. And I wasn't shocked. It was completely evident that my dreams, since the very beginning in Minneapolis, contained real details of Antwerp . . . that I'd been seeing Antwerp for real. It was also clear at that point that my dreams were happening when I was awake, which was terrifying—not that I was afraid—I was

---

horrified at how brutal, violent things were around me, things that I saw. Lurking soldiers in bars. Flemish kids crouched and eyeballing me with these cold blue eyes. I knew the outcome of Nazi warplanes shooting overhead and the Gestapo at the corner smoking and kids riding their bikes in the park. I knew what was coming. I knew it all. Professor Lewis would not have been afraid. He would've been . . . interested, would've wanted to get to the bottom of this. Cultural anthropologists have a lot of courage.

Yes, Barry, I could see stuff from the early forties and also from the fall of 2004. I could see it all simultaneously.

I didn't see the little dream girl on the street when I was awake. I didn't see my dad. Just 1940s stuff.

I would call these visions . . . Listen, Barry, call them what you want. Those in the medical profession would say I was having a psychotic break.

I didn't feel psycho. But I imagine most crazy people don't think they're crazy.

I don't think I was crazy.

I got locked up. Yup. I did a good job not reacting to things for a few days. But the park. That park. I couldn't stop myself. It was three a.m., and I wasn't asleep because my cough was getting worse. (Probably couldn't have slept even without the cough.) I was awake in my underpants, pacing around, scribbling in my notebook, when it came to me. That park. The one we walked into after the bakery? Stads Park. I understood . . . remembered (though I'd never been there, would have no way of remembering) that my father's childhood apartment was on one corner of that park. I realized I'd been dreaming of that park for six weeks. I knew exactly where the apartment was.

I don't know. I don't know. This stuff, which happens all the time to me, makes me dizzy . . . because it makes no sense and it makes complete sense, which is also why it doesn't make sense.

The doctor in Antwerp thought I was schizophrenic. At first. After we talked for a few days he didn't think so anymore.

It was quite a scene.

Journal Entry,
October 5, 2004, 3:12 a.m.

Dream park is no dream.

Light coming in from the window. You look down at the park in front of the apartment. Dark trees. The path where kids ride bikes during the day. In the corner of the park, an enormous sculpture, maybe of soldiers, bronze shining green in the streetlight. Window open, cold air, springtime, the trees with new leaves, leaves shaking because of oncoming soldiers and trucks and tanks.

The park you see from the apartment window is the park you sat in yesterday, eating a knish on a bench. It's that park.

Troops march past the park, down the street, past your apartment, and Belgians are with them, and it's not Dad, not Dad, the little girl in her broken English says it's not Dad, but someone is there in the apartment window when you recede into shadows, spotlights training the windows from the street below.

That's not Dad in the window. 1940s. He's in the apartment, with you, with the girl, cowering in the corner, shaking, crying. He's just a kid. Who is it in the window?

It's that park in your dreams. It's that street in your dreams. It's that apartment. The map says the street is Rubens Lei.

Go see it now.

Day Nine:
Transcript 3

Cranberry heard me run out of my room. I wasn't quiet about it. Yanked the door, slammed it, and took off running. Cranberry left his room across the hall from mine and tailed me onto the street. Out on the street he shouted at me. He caught up, but I wouldn't talk to him. Just ran toward the park. Cranberry chased behind, chattering God knows what.

From married father of three with a corporate job and . . . khakis . . . to jumping in the Seine . . . to racing down an Antwerp street at 3:30 in the morning, hacking out my lungs, wearing a T-shirt and underpants. Right?

(Laughs.) I don't remember the last time I really laughed. (Laughs.) Barry, I stormed the . . . I stormed my father's apartment. Poor Cranberry. Poor, poor Cranberry outside . . . hearing me screaming and glass breaking . . . (Laughs.)

You read the letters, Barry. I was sent to a nursing home after that.

Letter 39
October 10, 2004

Dearest Jack Nicholson, who won an Oscar for *One Flew Over the Cuckoo's Nest,*

I'm writing to tell you I'm like that little guy, your friend, in the movie. Except he commits suicide and I can't. I'm like him, because I need a brother, like you, to guide me, and I am, I think, really fucking nuts. I am also a magician.

Listen, Jack.

My dad lived here, in Antwerp, Belgium. It's possible I have ESP because I can see the past in the present. Also, I don't drown in rivers. I'm locked up in a damn home for old crows. I can't stop coughing. What do you think?

Dear Jack, what was your name in that movie? Randle? That might be it. I'm not like you. My name is Theodore, and I'm not pretending. I see stuff and maybe there is some genius here in my head.

Jack, I am sitting at a table in a common room in some kind of nursing home or rest home. Institutionalized, my man. And I wish the old ladies would turn down the TV so I can think. They can't understand me. The doctor just gave me a pill, but I'm not sleepy yet. I have ten minutes of consciousness and I'm going to use it.

Listen, Jack. I did something crazy. Rock star–sized crazy, which you might have done yourself, in a movie or in real life, because that's the kind of guy you are. This will sound familiar: broken glass, screaming, rock throwing. This all happened at the apartment building where my father grew up, so it wasn't a random crazy.

You weren't in World War II, were you, Jack? You're too young for that. There's some WWII stuff happening in my head and on the street and in that apartment building, which I've been dreaming for months, although I didn't know it was in Antwerp until I got in front of the apartment building and broke it wide open with a rock. The Belgians can't be pleased with me. The Jews in the building thought I was a North African terrorist, middle of the night, going to burn the place down to announce my hatred of Israel and of Jews in general.

Me? An Arab terrorist? Come on! I'm half-Jewish.

Okay, I'm getting sleepy. Here's what you need to know: I am in a rest home (a nursing home?) and I am resting my aching head and lungs. I am not free to go.

I'm surrounded by ancient crow women in bathrobes with no teeth who scream at me bloody murder in French and Flemish. They howl, Jack. And I tell them, "I can't help you. I'm an American. I have my own problems. Please watch TV." And the old women howl.

Why am I in a nursing home? I am criminally insane, I think. Like you pretended to be in the movie. You got shock treatment, right? Not me. Not yet. They shouldn't put me with all of these howling old women, though. What if I pick them up from their wheelchairs and throw them out the window? (I wouldn't do such a thing . . . our mother is in a home, Jack, just like this one, except in English—but how would the authorities know that if they think I'm criminally insane?) I should be in jail or in a serious mental institution with my brother (you!) and a tall Indian and we should play some basketball.

Not that I'm complaining. I don't want to be in a serious mental institution.

There was a police station at the beginning and a jail cell for a short time (I slept there for a couple of hours, bled a little on my shirt). But by noon the next day I was brought here, to this gravy-smelling, carpeted place, and was told to sleep, which seems very nice, considering I shattered the glass on that apartment building door, my dad's old apartment building, by throwing a large rock, considering how I wrenched open the door by reaching through broken glass for the handle and then sprinted through the lobby, bleeding, alarms blaring, then took an elevator up to the fifth floor and knew which one was THE apartment, DAD's apartment. I pounded on its door, shouted, "Open up," then tried to break down the door, while Cranberry screamed on the street for me to stop, cries getting more and more plaintive, and then other people screamed in other apartments and especially in the apartment where I pounded. And while I operated in present time, the 1940s tanks were rolling, the sirens blaring, gunshots up the street ricocheting, echoing, cracking in my ears.

This is not appropriate behavior. I should be jailed.

This behavior, however, seemed completely rational at the time (I needed to see if my dreams were true), and I remember the break-in perfectly. It confounds the doctor who visits me each day that I seem so rational. I remember thinking while trying to get in the apartment, "The people who live here won't open up with me screaming and bleeding like this. Better break down the door to get a look inside."

A look at what?

Jack Nicholson, get this: This apartment is THE apartment where my dead dad and his brother Solly grew up, at least until the war (WWII). I know this now to be true and fully believed, no, KNEW it to be true when I did my crime . . . though it was unconfirmed by outside sources, only the voices in my head, which are just thoughts, my thoughts. The owners of the apartment confirmed the fact for me when I was arrested, told Cranberry to tell me I got the right apartment—it was owned by a Rimberg—but went about contacting them in the WRONG way. Please tell him not to come back, they said to Cranberry, referring to me. I can't blame them.

And so I'm locked in a nursing home, without other men with whom to organize basketball games and fishing trips. I'm not going anywhere, Jack.

And with sedation there are no dreams, not even when I'm awake. And everything is getting dull and soft now. I like that. And I speak with a doctor who has a soft voice and a Flemish accent, and he scribbles notes and nods at me. He wants to see the notebooks I carry in my backpack. I tell him I will show them to him when I am more comfortable. I tell him that I'm writing a memoir and it's no big thing. He believes me and we are making progress. He, of course, will never see these notebooks. They are incriminating, Jack.

I have to take a nap.

Day Nine:
Transcript 4

Why *wouldn't* I write to Jack Nicholson?

I barely remember writing that letter.

Drugged up.

No, I wasn't scared in the home. Actually felt good there.

The doctor didn't ride me or push me. We had good talks. He asked a lot of the same questions you ask.

Do you have bad dreams? What's in your dreams? Do you have violent dreams? Do you know who you are, where you're from? Do you abuse substances? Do you think about God a lot?

I didn't tell him anything real—nothing about dreams or suicide or Nazis. I told him about my divorce and coming to Antwerp to find my father and how it had been a rough year. But I didn't tell him any of the story as it actually happened.

Well, I wouldn't have given you anything either, but you got to my backpack, Barry, to my notebooks.

You know . . . really that isn't true. I gave up the fight before I got to Green Bay. I probably would've told you.

The accident changed me, yes. But really, by the time I got here I was already changed.

Well, I'm not paranoid like I was in Antwerp, for one thing.

Maybe it wasn't paranoia—could've been rational. When I was in Antwerp, I knew anything I'd say about anything that was happening in my head or in my line of sight would sound delusional. I mean, I didn't even tell Cranberry about the dreams or visions . . . hallucinations is what a doctor would call them. Because I was fully aware I would sound ill . . . and I didn't want anyone telling me this intense stuff was just the product of my . . .

I don't think so, like I said. But I still wonder. We both wonder, don't we?

I don't blame you, Barry. I could have a mental illness. I might be crazy and also incredibly lucky . . . wildly, insanely, incredibly lucky, and I might float really well. That could be my whole deal. This whole deal, including the accident—it could just be a combination of crazy and lucky.

The doctor didn't think I was crazy. We went to work. We talked about my failed marriage, how I failed in it. He told me that love is an action, not a feeling. And if I love someone, I had better act on that or love is meaningless. That's right up my alley, that kind of talk. That sounded smart. If you love, you act on it.

After a week of seeing me, the doctor thought I'd been sleep deprived, that's all. And stressed out, I guess.

You really think so? *Totally* delusional? Why?

Uncle Charley?

I guess it's strange I wrote him. But I watched a lot of *My Three Sons* in the early eighties. Uncle Charley made me feel safe.

Big shocks coming, yes.

Letter 40
October 11, 2004

Dear Uncle Charley,

You know what, old man? I haven't seen my uncle Solly in so long, I realize I've begun to think Solly looks like you (whoever you are who played Uncle Charley on *My Three Sons,* which I watched on WGN). My uncle Solly is a jackass, I believe. You, Uncle Charley, were kind of a jackass on that show, gruff, grunty old man. But at least you had a tender heart, a heart of gold, and you wore an apron and cooked food for poor vulnerable Ernie, who was an orphan or something and who wore big nerd glasses and was sad, and who I totally identified with.

I have family news, Uncle. You should make some brisket. We should sit down at the kitchen table and talk.

It is Monday. The Yiddish weekly came out today. And I made the papers! You must be very proud. Kaatje and Cranberry hurried over here to the home to show me this paper, which I appreciate. Those two are good kids, though they don't know the value of money.

They were on their way to lunch, to a Vietnamese restaurant they've grown to love (oh do they talk about this restaurant), minding their own business, when they saw the Yiddish newspaper on a stand outside a Jewish paper shop. Big headline! RIMBERG in big big letters on the front page of a paper filled almost entirely with Hebrew characters! So instead of eating at the Vietnamese restaurant (on my dime for the third time in three days), they bought the paper (with my money) and ran over here to the rest home to show me. It really is impressive, too, this headline. It ends in an exclamation, Uncle Charley. It says something like:

RIMBERG GSCHFINCTER!

Problem: none of us can read Yiddish. Certainly I can't and Kaatje—who left her job to help me and Cranberry negotiate this foreign place, which is very sweet of her (although a little pricey for me)—can't read Yiddish, although she was perfectly sure she could read Yiddish the other day, before she was asked to read it. The article is certainly about me, though. It refers to me, Theodore Rimberg, by name. And more interestingly, it lists four other Rimberg names in roman characters: Sol Rimberg, Josef Rimberg, Aida Rimberg, Laurence Rimberg. Uncle, Father, Grandmother, Grandfather, I think, though I don't know the last two names. We know Solly and Josef, don't we?

The only Rimberg not mentioned is dear brother David, who broke his contract and was asked to leave the show. So sorry, David! Persona non grata. Bet he wishes he hadn't been such a pain to work with! Hindsight.

Because we could not read the Yiddish newspaper, Kaatje and Cranberry ran off with the copy they brought to me, and they're going to go to the train station where they are hoping to find some English-speaking Hasid to translate the article for them. I don't think they'll have any problem doing so. There are English-speaking Hasids on every corner in that neighborhood. I thought they should contact the newspaper and ask for an English translation. (This is the advice you would've given too, Uncle Charley, while you listened to our problems and served us dinner in your apron.) Kaatje thought that would take too long. Why go make phone calls when the streets are filled with English-speaking Hasids? That's fair. She's a smart girl. Let her take care of this business.

In other news, Dear Uncle: I'm not exactly a prisoner.

When Cranberry was leaving a couple of moments ago he whispered, "You look better. You feeling better?"

I said, "I've never felt better. Sleep is important."

He said, then, "You can come with us . . . I mean you have to come back here in a couple of hours . . . but we could take you with us right now if you want."

Kaatje heard him say this to me, though she was away at the front desk, speaking to the fat cow that sits there, asking for the quickest route to get to the train station. Kaatje has good ears. She shot Cranberry angry eyes. She shook her head, no.

"No thank you," I said. "I'm not going anyplace but back to bed."

I'm not stupid, Uncle Charley. I don't want to go out on those streets. I appreciate the little white pills that keep me sleeping through the night. I like my bed and the couches. Truth is, I'm scared shitless to leave this place. I'm certainly not ready for the mean streets of the Shtetl, and I don't want to see any more Nazis. I am not interested in that.

I am, however, interested to find out what's so big about me that I should make the newspaper! I suppose it's an account of my criminal behavior. But why the fat headline?

I am also interested in taking a nap. When I wake up, we might know more.

Will report, good Uncle. You can count on that. I'll come downstairs and you'll have baked some cookies and we'll have a chat.

T.

Letter 41
October 11, 2004

Dear Uncle Charley,

I need advice. How do I negotiate this? Help me.

One of the howling little women next to the television set was delivered a Yiddish newspaper. I pointed out the article on the front page and said, "That's me! I'm Rimberg." The woman, who was dressed in a dressing gown and had thin painted blond hair and eyebrows painted crookedly in dogshit brown on her face, began to scream and howl, which wasn't a shock like it might have been if these women hadn't howled at me for the last seven days. But this howling was different than the howling before. Generally if I'm stern enough in my voice, I can make the women stop howling. But this new howling, this woman wouldn't stop, and she howled and screamed even though I told her very sternly to be quiet. My stern tones only seemed to fuel her howling, and soon I realized that her howl was terribly specific, even with my hands covering my ears, because she howled, "Rimberg," and she pointed at me. Then I became upset and shouted, "Cut that infernal racket out, or I will push you down the stairs," which didn't do any good, because she speaks no English and has clearly lost her mind. And then, with the one arm she has that hasn't been destroyed or atrophied by some stroke in her past, she attempted to wheel herself away from me . . . but of course, owing to the physics of wheelchairs, she was only able to wheel herself around and around in circles. Whenever her eyes landed upon me, she would howl terribly, her level of terror increasing with every turn. And she often howled, "Rimberg."

This cyclical howling, which fell outside the pattern of the everyday howling, captured the attention of the other guests, and they came to find out what the matter was. She screamed,

"Rimberg," and pointed at me, which set most of them into a complete state. Several screamed at me in French and shuffled toward me in their slippers, pointing and slicing the air with their bony fingers.

I was so afraid, Uncle Charley! I screamed. It was a horror film. My own scream finally brought the Flemish cow from behind her desk down the hall to assist me. Other staff followed.

It was too late. One howling woman had fallen to her knees in front of me, still screaming in French, veins bursting in her temples. She had grabbed the arms of my chair, and the staff could not pry her off, her adrenaline prevented them from moving her. Her breath in my nostrils smelled of fish. I shook my head and said, "American. I don't understand French." And so she spoke English. "You . . . you . . . murderer. Mother. Father. Sister. Family. All! Butcher!" she cried. Her ancient saliva sprayed me.

The staff finally managed to remove her bony fingers from around the arms of my chair, and she wept and others wept, and they repeated "Rimberg" as they wept.

I fear, Dear Uncle, our family hasn't the best reputation in this city.

I am locked in my room now. Staff tells me I need to stay in my room, because I am upsetting the other patients. I told them I would lock myself in my room and had no interest in being with these crazy women.

Could these women kill me in the night? Would they have the strength? I cannot die at the hands of these howling women. What do you think? What's your advice? Do you have any knitting needles stored in your apron I can borrow for protection?

No one has permission to kill me but me, and even I can't do that.

Won't someone save me?

T.

Day Nine:
Transcript 5

As I said, Father, I get attacked every time I'm in a hospital.

Nobody would explain to me what was going on, which was so disheartening.

Well . . . I'd seen the doctor in the morning, and it had gone well. I'd been in the place almost a week, and I was feeling good. I coughed less. The doctor and I discussed strategies for dealing with anxiety, strategies that would help me think rationally while dealing with stress. After the craziness of Paris and the break-in, I was receptive to this behavioral therapy . . . I wanted to be anchored and rational. So things were good.

Yes. I wrote letters to fictional people. So?

Of course the doctor didn't know. He told me I was doing very well, and I felt like I was . . . even if I was writing to . . .

Who the hell else was I going to write to?

Sorry, Father Barry. But really. Who?

No. Kaatje and Cranberry didn't come back. Abandoned, that's what I thought. Read the journal.

Journal Entry,
October 11, 10 p.m.

Nick Kelly. Cranberry. With payment comes responsibility. I pay you and you are responsible to me, responsible for my well-being. And I need some help now, Nick Kelly. I have to hide in a room while you and your girlfriend are out eating at restaurants? Meanwhile, I'm being stabbed in the throat by an old woman with her knitting needle, which might really happen? How is this equitable? Why should I be left to the bony wolves while you spend my money?

Day Nine:
Transcript 6

I don't know why I was fixated on money. Reading over this stuff, now . . . I think I sound like my dad.

No, they didn't. Things were happening on the outside I didn't know about.

I got the envelope with the Irish ferry ticket.

Yes, a different side of the story was coming out in the home, too.

Letter 42
October 12, 2004

Dear Uncle Charley,

I would like to leave this place. I don't like it here anymore. If Cranberry ever comes back, I'll ask him to take me away.

All night last night I suffered not from the nightmares of a past I don't understand, but from waking fears of howling old Jewish mothers sneaking into my room, poking me in the face with their needlepoint needles. Every noise made me jump out of bed.

The ladies are crazy and inconsistent, and I don't understand.

The morning staff made me go to breakfast in the common room. It seems there was no note left for the morning staff to tell them about the violence of yesterday, and even though I demanded I get breakfast in my room, I was not allowed.

I snuck to the common room and breathed relief. I was the first to arrive and was able to choose my own seat, where I could face the door.

The old ladies arrived one-by-one or in pairs, pushing their walkers or being rolled in wheelchairs. None would sit by me, but gathered around the other large table. Thankfully they did not howl or scream, but only glared and shook their heads. They fit eleven, some in wheelchairs, at a round table meant for no more than eight. That is my revenge on them. They had to reach for their food. Now their dressing gowns are covered in yogurt and orange juice from their shaking hands.

But maybe I shouldn't want revenge. Not on all of them.

Listen to this. As I was finishing my yogurt and fruit and coffee, a tiny bent little woman began to shuffle toward me from the entryway. I drank my coffee and eyeballed her, worried. I had a last bite of yogurt. Still she shuffled toward me. Adrenaline surged, and I prepared to fend her off by hitting her with my breakfast plates. But she did not take up an aggressive stance. Rather, as she got to me, she began to smile so broad, and her eyes crinkled and became wet with joy, and I could see she must have been a great beauty.

She said, "Please?" pointing to the chair next to me, asking if she could sit.

I looked over to the table of hateful howling women. They were busy spilling on themselves and seemed in no mood to ambush me while I talked to this woman. So I said, "Please," and smiled, although I was quite nervous.

She sat slow. I braced her by the bony elbow as she bent her knees, quaking, finally falling the last foot to the metal seat of the chair. Once in her chair, she put her tiny hand on my forearm. It was a warm touch on my forearm, gentle, and I felt certain she was crazy and had mistaken me for her son or husband. But she said, "Rimberg."

At which I gasped.

She peered at me and touched my face, then nodded, scratched her chin, rolled her eyes. She said, "Hm. English," and laughed and shook her head. "My English . . . is no good."

I nodded. I said, "It's okay."

She held up her hand. She said, "Father? Rimberg? He took mother and me from the train, yes?"

"I'm sorry," I said, assuming this was the beginning of the bad news about our family, the news that caused the howling women to hate me—that we wouldn't let people ride on our train.

"No," she smiled. "This terrible war. Father"—she pointed at me—"took mother"—she pointed at herself, nodding—"and me from train." She paused again, nodded, smiled, closed her eyes, and with an extended S sound, she said, "Saved. From train."

"My father?" I shook my head. "No. He was a child during the war. Second World War?"

"Yes!" she nodded. "Child!" She smiled, her eyes lighting.

"Okay," I said. "Thank you," I told her. "That's very nice of you." I stood, uncomfortable, ready to go.

She smiled and nodded. "Saved from Nazis," she said.

"Okay," I said. "My father? Okay."

She smiled and nodded. She stayed in her chair, quiet but smiling, waiting for her breakfast to be delivered. I stood next to her for a moment. The howlers were staring at us. One of them shouted something. Then this little tiny sweet woman spit out in staccato French, pointing at me. Some of the howlers slowly began to nod at me, but others shook their heads no and shouted back. All the while my tiny, pretty, sweet old woman kept pointing at me and talking loudly.

After a moment, I bowed a little and left. A couple of the howlers waved.

I have no idea what took place during breakfast. It's all strange, Uncle. I need more rest. I need quiet. There is civil unrest in this home based on my presence here, a now divided group of elderly women. There is tension.

Really, Uncle Charley (I wish you were really my uncle, or that I was actually writing my real uncle), if my administrative staff would come back for me, I'd be gone today, right now. Unfortunately I have no idea where they are, and my calls to the hotel to find them go unreturned. Things could get bad for me if I don't get some relief. The doctor yesterday told me I'm in pretty good shape mentally, much better than he would've imagined, and I agreed with him then . . . I haven't dreamt for days and I feel much like myself. Or rather, felt much like myself. But this is frightening, and I fear I won't be okay for long.

I need rest. I need information. I'd like to know if I'm a criminal or a hero. I need to know. I want to leave.

Why am I writing to you?

Journal Entry,
October 12, 2004

A ticket. Crinkled. Ferry. Rosslare, Ireland, to Cherbourg, France. The date is June 17, 1990.

On the back: "How is it I love you so much?" That's my handwriting. I wrote it in 1990.

On the back: "Are you still such a romantic? What are you doing here, T.?" The message is in a woman's handwriting. The ink is fresh.

This came in an envelope that was delivered to my room by the fat cow nurse. She said a woman in a black skirt with black hair—the nurse gestured curly with her hand, and at first I took it to mean crazy—left it for me at the lobby.

There is no name, no phone number, no address.

But I know.

Julia Hilfgott.

Letter Faxed to Fr. Barry McGinn, August 17, 2005

Note hand-written in top margin: *This is the only correspondence I received. Thank you so much for the news about T., strange as it was. I feared the worst. Please let me know if I can be of further assistance. — Sincerely, Julia Mendez*

October 12, 2004

Julia,

You know, of course, that I am confused.

Look at the evidence. I'm incarcerated in a nursing home for ancient and angry Jewish women. This I still find confusing, but less confusing now that I know you met my administrative staff on the morning of my arrest. Why didn't you reveal yourself to them? Who did you need to convince to keep me out of jail? Thank you. Thank you for this. If it weren't for the controversy I'm causing in this home, I would gladly stay here forever.

Julia, I am confused. What are you doing here? You live in Antwerp? My administrative staff tells me you live next door to the building where my father grew up. I find that amazing and, of course, completely appropriate to our short relationship. Did you know my father? If so, why didn't you contact me? He apparently knew where I lived, though he gave me no indication he was alive until the time of his death, when he sent me some letters.

Will you see me, Julia? Please? I could use a sane voice.

Can I come see you, so you don't have to go out of your way? (You already have, but I want to take some responsibility.)

I'm sending Cranberry (purple hair). Please send word back.

T.

Day Nine:
Transcript 7

You've spoken to Julia? She's okay?

Did you talk to her about everything that happened in Antwerp?

Good. I'm glad she verified it. I know the stories are hard to believe. Even if I'm mentally ill, I'm not that crazy.

It wasn't romantic between us this time. Not at all. Things change.

Yes. Julia makes me think . . . makes me think life isn't random. I mean—her showing up . . . When she walked into the waiting room, the light intensified.

Me and Julia are connected. And it wasn't romantic.

You're helping me tremendously, Barry . . . I guess . . . starting in Poland, during the winter, I just stopped all thinking. I haven't reflected at all on this. I stopped thinking. Thank you for helping me.

Julia did know my father.

No, not when I was with her in 1990. She didn't live in Antwerp then. She was visiting.

She didn't know him well. Her husband sued Dad's business once.

Within an hour of Julia coming to get me, she and I were in a restaurant and I was sobbing, and Julia was holding me, because she'd told me that Dad had died, that it had been in the early summer, two months before I received his letters. He'd had cancer, and it was fast. It was in the papers. I could have figured it out on the Internet, actually. I kept saying to her that I should have known he was dead since he sent an inheritance . . . but it wasn't an inheritance exactly, there was nothing legal-seeming about the check, and the letters he sent with the money sounded so present . . . so I thought he wasn't dead.

Yes, I was really crushed. For whatever reason, I did really believe Dad was alive, even though I repeatedly called him my dead dad. I hoped. When she told me, I apologized to Dad, you know, "I'm so sorry, Dad. I'm so sorry." It really didn't make sense considering he left me . . . but I thought he'd been calling for me, maybe, with the dreams.

Poor Julia kept apologizing while I cried. She thought I knew where Dad was all these years. She was always afraid she'd run into me in Antwerp. She didn't want to see me.

The news couldn't have come from a better source. Julia makes me feel in my skin. I needed family. I wrote in the journal someplace that Julia must've been my sister in a past life.

After breaking the news, she walked with me for hours, pointed out where Dad's business was (and it's still there—his partners bought him out in the spring before he died . . . well, sort of). She sent Cranberry and Kaatje for my stuff and put me up in her apartment for a few days. Then she set up this thing with Mrs. Fisher.

Julia's husband was in the apartment. Of course. Mendez. He's a very good guy.

Yes. I knew she was pregnant. I knew . . . I think before she did.

Is the baby healthy?

Good.

A photo?

Look at that hair! That's Julia's hair!

Letter 43
October 15, 2004

Dear David,

I don't have anyone else to tell.

Do you remember Julia Hilfgott, Julia from Dublin in 1990? You called me an idiot for leaving her. Remember? Well, you were probably right. Julia's here.

You don't know where here is. You were such an ass to me a couple of months ago (you've been such an ass to me forever), so I didn't tell you I left the U.S. for good.

I'm back in Antwerp, where Dad lived (although we didn't know it) and Julia lives here. She saved me from going to jail.

I broke into the apartment building where Dad and Solly grew up. Julia convinced the authorities to put me in a private rest home and to have me psychologically evaluated. Julia apparently had to work hard to keep me out of jail. She was there when I broke in because she lives in the building next door to Dad's old place. She heard the glass crashing and police sirens and ran outside and recognized me.

Two days ago Julia managed to get me out of the home. She told me she knew Dad and she told me he died. Sorry, David.

I wanted answers. That's why I'm here. I wanted to know why Dad left us, where Dad went. There are lots of secrets. It's opened up a new world, this investigation. Julia introduced me to an old woman named Mrs. Fisher who grew up across the hall from our family. I got my answers, and I think I should give them to you.

This isn't an easy decision. When Charlie was born, I called you, and you said, "Good luck with that." That's all. But I am preparing to tell you what I know. This is your family, too.

T.

Day Nine:
Transcript 8

Has Julia told you any of this?

Okay. Well, Kaatje and Cranberry were confused. They were at the police station, of course, the morning of my break-in. And there was Julia arguing vehemently with a whole crowd of people who wanted my head for causing such a disturbance. And everyone knew who I was, because I look a lot like my dad. Kaatje and Cranberry didn't know what was going on. Why did people know me? Who was this woman? How did she know so much about me? Confusing.

When they asked her, Julia would only tell them she knew me through my dad. They asked her to talk to me. She refused, made them promise not to tell me that she was involved or even in Antwerp. Kaatje and Cranberry were so confused, but they agreed not to tell. They were worried I'd get put in jail if they revealed her identity.

No. Julia had no interest in seeing me. I didn't know the impact I'd had on her when we were so young. She thought she'd found her true love, her soul mate . . . and I disappeared from Antwerp without saying goodbye. She was devastated. You know, she was twenty-two then. Twenty-two is tough. It put her into a deep depression.

Julia and I are a lot alike, except she's always known herself and has managed to keep working to do what she wants to do, instead of falling to pieces and starting over every couple of years like I did.

She believed she'd never forgive me for what I did.

Dramatic, yes. But true, I think.

It was only after Kaatje and Cranberry came to her with the Yiddish newspaper article that Julia agreed to get involved further. Cranberry told her I was searching for Dad. She couldn't believe I didn't know he'd died. It broke her heart . . . she's dramatic. She decided she had a responsibility to get me information. Not because I was me, but because people deserve to know what happened to their parents. European Jews are very big on this recovery of history, I think. Julia knew Mrs. Fisher well.

I had to write David. Who else was there? My kids are too young to understand. I'll tell them someday.

An act of forgiveness? I don't know. I mean, I'm not a great person. David's not a great person. Neither of us deserves anything. I just thought he should know, even if he doesn't have any interest in knowing. At least I gave him the opportunity— or would have had I sent him the letters. And . . . I almost didn't tell him everything.

Letter 44
October 15, 2004

David,

I'm writing you from a balcony overlooking Stads Park. This is Julia Hilfgott's apartment, which is adjacent to the apartment where our father spent the first ten years of his life. Strange?

I've been told it is not so strange. The Jews in Antwerp live in the same neighborhoods they always have since the beginning of time, clustered a bit by sect. Julia knows dozens of families who have lived in all of the buildings along this street, this park. This is what I've been told, though I suppose I still find the coincidence unfathomable. But there aren't that many buildings, and there aren't that many Jews of our family's kind, modern Conservative Jews.

There are people in this neighborhood who knew our family and remember them well. One old lady in particular, Mrs. Fisher. Mrs. Fisher lived across the hall from our family. She still lives in that apartment, across from where I pounded on our father's door. She remembers everything.

She doesn't know everything, though. Mrs. Fisher, for instance, had no idea our father had children, certainly not goyische children. How everything has changed, she said.

But she knows a lot. And now she knows even more—she's even been a first-hand witness to my emergence onto this scene. Mrs. Fisher nearly had a heart attack that night—breaking glass, screaming man. My assistant, Cranberry, screaming in the street. I caused her bad memories. She thought it was the Gestapo waking her up at three a.m.

Can't blame Mrs. Fisher for feeling ambivalent about me. Can't blame her for her anger toward our grandfather, either— she hates him. And that's fair, David. He wasn't a good man.

Luckily Mrs. Fisher is lonely, and her desire to talk to someone, anyone, even the enemy, outweighed her ambivalence about me.

Are we the enemy? Not you and me, David. Not really, except that I woke her up. Grandfather certainly.

Maybe someday I'll tell you about the ancient howling ladies at the rest home. They knew exactly who I was, David. It was in the Yiddish newspaper. It was alive in their graying memories. They knew I was our grandfather's grandson.

Laurence, our father's father, was a powerful man. He became the president of the largest synagogue in the city. He was a very very rich man. Not from diamonds, though, which is what I thought.

What did our grandfather, a poor Polish immigrant, whom we never met, who died before the end of World War II, do to get filthy rich?

He was a steel importer and exporter. He became wealthy by making contracts with the German government after the First World War. In a way, he helped rebuild the Reich (sort of). He helped rebuild German productive capacity and then purchased iron and steel products from them and exported them all over Europe and to Latin America. Yes, he helped build the Third Reich, but only in a physical sense. And not many in Antwerp believe Grandfather could see into the future, see what devastation was coming from the Nazis he did business with after 1933 (Mrs. Fisher actually believes he could see into the future).

Here's what Mrs. Fisher said (imagine a tiny and bent Gabor sister, her voice like Eva in *The Aristocats*): "Your grandfather knew something. He always knew something before everyone else knew anything. He was magic, because he always understood what would happen before it happened. That's why he was so respected. And feared, too. Sure feared. That's why others accepted his investment in their businesses even when it came at such a price. He knew what would happen before it happened."

But we're not to the terrible secrets yet, David. Grandfather was not terrible because he could possibly see into the future and was a tough businessman and had business dealings with the Nazis before the war. His perfidy to the Jews was much worse. Our grandfather was a terrible traitor.

We spent the afternoon with Mrs. Fisher. Julia, me, and my two assistants were sitting at a table on Mrs. Fisher's balcony. It was a gray day, as most are here, but the air felt good and we could see bikers and walkers, Hasids and Indians, moving past on the street below. It was an important day.

I took pages and pages of notes. I'll copy them and send them to you, I think.

Mrs. Fisher prepared much food for our meeting. She served tea and scampi and iced water with lemon, and then cake and finger pastries and coffee, and then wine. And then, after hours, some other kind of fish, as it moved toward late afternoon and we all were losing energy. She enjoyed having company, even me, and clearly enjoyed telling her stories, speaking about these ghosts from her past. I haven't ever had a meal prepared like that.

I just thought of something, David. I'll write this when I can. I have something to do first.

T.

Dear Julia Child,

I just heard you died a couple of months ago. I'm sorry. When I was a kid, I'd turn on Public Television looking for *Sesame Street* or the *The Electric Company,* and I'd find you, cooking and smiling. You sounded like a Muppet, a chicken caricature of a New Englander. Bok bok bok. You caught my attention. In my own kitchen, there was always one lightbulb out in the ceiling fixture. It was always dim in there as my mother made another box of macaroni. On the television, you laughed and wore colorful blouses and whooped and clucked while preparing some kind of chicken, while discussing the proper wine to drink with it. I couldn't take my eyes off you. Do you know how much we've lost?

T. Rimberg

Day Nine:
Transcript 9

Sitting in that building, on that balcony, eating in that way with people all around . . . it felt like I was part of a family. This is how my dad and his parents spent free time, on these balconies, eating, talking. There was no TV to baby-sit the kids.

It was an odd combination. In some respects, I felt so good sitting out there. I felt something about what was right with my family before I was born. At the same time, this terrible history, which can't entirely be blamed on my grandfather . . . I mean, he didn't create the Nazis . . . was being revealed.

It was a strange thing to do, to write Julia Child. I guess I needed to acknowledge something right in the way they lived.

Dear David,

We're ghosts from the past. Here are Mrs. Fisher's thoughts, written from my notes of our conversation. Get ready.

Mrs. Fisher was born in February of 1925. The next month our Uncle Solly was born in the apartment across the hall.

One of Mrs. Fisher's earliest memories was listening to our grandfather verbally bludgeon our grandmother, Aida. "Your grandmother wanted to have a real house. And sure Laurence could afford a house! But he would not pay for a house staff and said there was too much room already—it was a very nice apartment, still very nice, you should look in. I was in the park with my mother and the governess and your grandmother and uncle. Your grandfather happened on us as he walked home from his business, and he screamed at Aida that he would not pay for a house, not ever. I don't know why this memory is so vivid. Perhaps his viciousness?"

Mrs. Fisher remembers her mother calling Grandfather a low-class shtetler who couldn't spend his mountain of money because he might not have enough for his potatoes. I don't understand exactly what that means, David.

Grandfather was not interested in having another child. People talked about Rimberg and his one child and thought, what must be wrong with Aida if there is only one child? Of course, another Rimberg did arrive, eventually. Mrs. Fisher says Grandfather knew before Grandma Aida did. "You're pregnant," Mrs. Fisher remembers him spitting in the hall, looking at her hips and shaking his head.

"No!" Grandma Aida spat back. "I would know if I am with child!"

Eight months later, in late 1928, our father, Josef, was born.

This child, though, this special child, he softened Laurence up. Dad was so beautiful, light brown curly hair from the beginning (like yours, Mrs. Fisher said to me), these blue eyes like his father's (she pointed at my face, my eyes, and nodded). An angel of a child. "I was not even four years old, but I remember this change in your grandfather. Never did I see him shout at your grandmother again." Mrs. Fisher nodded.

And then, David, there was more talk: steel, and our grandmother's purchasing of apartments and also constructing them, building her own little empire of real estate. They prospered even through the economic strife of the thirties, with trips to the ocean in summer, Knokke on the North Sea, afternoon tea with the Conservative Association Antwerp families sitting together at luxury hotels. Grandfather rose to be president of the Conservative Association and to the head of many committees at Van den Nestlei, the main synagogue, the most important in Antwerp, amid fraying nerves about what was happening in Germany.

This is when our grandfather began to commit real crimes, I think.

In January 1938 there was a meeting at the synagogue where our grandfather told everyone to calm down. Germany would not make the mistake of coming into Belgium again.

But in April of 1938 our grandfather, seemingly without reason, sent thirteen-year-old Solly to live with distant relatives in New York. Mrs. Fisher was brokenhearted. She'd believed she and Solly would grow up together, would marry, have children, walk them in carriages in the park, own a summer home in Knokke. Mrs. Fisher listened at her door as a Flemish man pulled Solly's trunk from the apartment. Solly and Grandfather stood in the hall. "Go," Grandfather told Solly. "Don't look back. Never speak of the past. Don't think of us anymore."

"Why would he say this if he didn't know what was coming?" Mrs. Fisher asked.

In 1939, Mrs. Fisher's father, nervous about moves Grandfather was making, sent her and her mother to Switzerland, where they stayed through the war. Mrs. Fisher's father was deported in 1942 and died in Auschwitz. Even writing that makes me sick.

In February of 1940 our father, Josef, disappeared from Antwerp. He didn't show up in school. He missed his music lessons, which he wouldn't ever do, because he was a very dedicated young pianist. When asked, Grandfather told everyone he'd sent his son to boarding school in Switzerland. In fact, people found out later, Dad was sent only a short distance away to Mechelen, to live with a liberal Catholic family whom Grandfather knew through business ties. Dad lived as a Catholic on a farm, where he survived the war.

Three months later, in May of 1940, the Germans came. Many in the community had escaped days in advance, having heard terrible stories of the treatment of Jews in Germany and in the already conquered Poland and Czechoslovakia. Of the some 50,000 Jews of Antwerp, about 25,000 remained behind, including our grandfather and grandmother.

The Germans set up an organization called the Judenrat to act as an intermediary between the Jewish community and the German leaders. Our grandfather, naturally, having done business in Germany and being fluent in German and a leader in the community, was chosen to lead the organization. Or rather, he volunteered to lead it. "He wanted to protect his business interests. Do you think he would just give away these holdings? All of the apartments your grandmother owned? No! So work with the Germans! They will reward people who cooperate."

And for a time, the Germans were hands-off. The Judenrat communicated German decrees to the Jews, and complained to the Germans if they felt their rights were being stepped on too much. (Why should we register? Why can't we visit the parks? Why should we wear these stars?) Complaints were actually heard and dealt with in rational conversations, although, of course, the Germans implemented the policies anyway. But with each day of seeming peace, and a continued "correct" attitude on the part of the Germans, Grandfather's reputation as leader grew. "Just obey obey obey. The Germans have no problem with us as long as we obey."

Then in April of 1941, Belgian anti-Semitic groups attacked the Jewish neighborhoods, burning businesses and homes. And the Germans did nothing to protect the Jews.

"The Germans will work with the Antwerp government to see that we are reimbursed," Grandfather told everyone. There was no reimbursement.

In early 1942, young people, young women and men, began to be called by the Germans to go to Germany to work. People came running to the Judenrat. "What should we do?"

"Obey," Grandfather told them. "It will be fine."

A lucky few, David, didn't obey. A few escaped right then. The ones who obeyed . . . You can imagine the consequences.

And in the summer of 1942, mass deportations began. Grandfather helped organize the movement. He called on groups of Jews to gather their belongings and meet at the train station, telling everyone it would be fine. Soon word came from Mechelen (remember Mechelen?) that a kind of transport depot had been set up there, and Jews from Brussels and Holland were being shoved into cars like cattle and hauled off to the east. It will be fine, our grandfather told everyone. It will be fine. And on August 27, 1942, there was a massive arrest, which took 70 percent of the Jews in Antwerp. Grandfather helped organize that, too, calling out from a megaphone to go peaceably. All the way into early 1943, even with horrible evidence mounting, our grandfather continued to collaborate with the Germans, continued to bring Jews to the square in front of this ornate train station in central Antwerp that has haunted me since I've been here. He stuck them on trains, and they were taken to Mechelen, put in cattle cars and hauled off to die. That's our grandfather, David. That's Laurence Rimberg.

In August of 1943, there were no Jews left, except for a few with Belgian citizenship and the members of the Judenrat. The Germans disbanded the Judenrat at that point, because, of course, there was no more need for an intermediary. The members of the Judenrat were rounded up on September 4, except—guess who? Laurence Rimberg. He had disappeared.

And here history gets hazy. Word on the street was that Grandfather had been working to get forged papers, a forged identity, for the year preceding the termination of the Judenrat. He, like Dad, was sandy-haired and could pass for a gentile easily. Our grandparents became Catholics who lived in Holland. They attended mass, so the story goes. They even became involved in social committees. But then Grandmother found Grandfather hanging from a beam in their tiny house (either hanged by his own hand, or perhaps not—there are plenty of rumors that suggest someone else did this). Shortly thereafter, our lovely grandmother Aida died. By the middle of 1944, although they didn't know it, Solly and Dad were orphans.

I've had dreams, David, of children being dragged by soldiers, dreams of our father laughing while watching the Jews be gathered. I've cowered in the corner in these dreams crying and terrified. It was our grandfather. He did this. We should be cursed.

There. You have the history.

T.

Dear Paul McCartney,

I'm in Julia's apartment and she's playing your music. *Take a sad song and make it better*. I don't know how, Paul. I don't have words. My dad is dead. All these people die. John is dead and George is dead. Linda is dead.

I've read about you riding that school bus and seeing George for the first time, him dressed like a fifties rockabilly hipster. You didn't want to talk to him, because he was only fourteen and you were older, and you rode the bus to school for weeks, aware of him, thinking about him. But you wouldn't play the fool. Eventually he sat down next to you on the bus and he said, *I play guitar*, and you nodded. You knew already. Then you brought him to John and the miracle happened.

And then John got divorced, and Julian, his son, was alone, so you wrote him "Hey Jules" and then turned it into "Hey Jude" and said to him *don't carry the world upon your shoulders*. My dad left me. I left my son. I have wanted to be dead.

My dad, when he was George's age on that school bus, tried to carry the world on his shoulders. A couple of months after you were born, in 1942, my dad tried to fix it. But it was something that couldn't really be fixed.

My beautiful friend Julia is back in the apartment someplace listening to you sing on a CD, Paul. I have to tell my brother.

T. Rimberg

Letter 48
October 15, 2004

David,

I'm sorry I left my last letter when I did. I had to stop. We are the grandkids of a monster. There is something else, though.

The howling women at the rest home didn't all hate me because of Grandfather. Some loved me because of Dad.

Dad was living on a farm with Catholics. The farm was in Mechelen (yes, that Mechelen, the same). Remember, he was sent there in 1940 when he was eleven, so he'd be saved even though the rest of Antwerp wouldn't be. From the farm where he stayed and went to school, ate and slept, Dad and his Catholic brothers (a fourteen-year-old and a sixteen-year-old) who were actual brothers and the sons of the man who took Dad in, watched the construction of the "transit depot" the Nazis set up. It was near the farm. Once it was finished and put into use, they likely heard screams floating across the green fields. They maybe could hear the pounding of cattle car floorboards, the crying of mothers and babies.

Dad and his brothers watched, and I guess they couldn't bear it. They thought they could fix it. With another friend, another child, some day in late summer in 1942, the three Catholic boys and our dad, all children, got on farm horses and descended on a train filled with Jews. They were armed with old farm rifles. I imagine they'd watched Hollywood westerns. They attacked the trains with scarves covering their faces.

David, these four boys killed the train engineer and killed the three guards on board. Dad flung open train doors, blood flowing, fire rising in his face. He freed the Jews on board, who all disappeared into the countryside. Most survived the war, including an old lady I met in the home. The fires the boys set destroyed the train, which blocked the tracks for several days so no other trains could come. During this attack, all three of Dad's friends were killed. Only Dad, our almost fourteen-year-old dad, lived. I don't know if he returned to the farm—how could he, the two sons dead? I don't know if he hid or what happened to him after that. But he survived, and so did the Jews on the train, around a hundred and fifty people. Millions died in the camps, but not this trainload. And then he came to America, and he married our mom and drove around the Midwest with a suitcase full of diamonds listening to eight-track tapes, and we're his sons. Isn't it strange?

Word got back to Antwerp. People here know what he did. If he hadn't returned to Antwerp in the late seventies, if he hadn't behaved poorly (I remember he hit you), our dad would still be considered a hero. He is a hero.

Charlie, Kara, and Sylvie are likely waking up right now, back in Minneapolis. Maybe they're having breakfast right now, or maybe watching public television. They are the grandchildren of a child-hero, the great-grandchildren of a monster. They are also my children.

David. You're my brother. I'm writing to you. I must love you.

T.

History shapes people. I had no history.

I don't know. Knowing the history of my grandfather might have made me darker. So sure Dad hid it. Probably thought he was protecting us from it. So he hid everything and disappeared. But secrets just leave this empty space. Knowing Dad's history might have given me courage.

No. I wasn't protected.

I'm not protecting my family now. I'm a runaway, too.

Not knowing Dad's history is no excuse.

That's enough, Barry.

Journal Entry,
October 18, 2004

Why is it a big deal? Why do I care about this business?

But I want to know. I want to know what this business was, why it was a big deal to Dad, a big enough deal that he disappeared and never came back. Mendez says it incorporated in 1980, soon after Dad turned into a ghost.

This ghost Dad was in Antwerp when I was here in 1990. We were likely close, blocks apart. We might have been in the same building.

I want to see this business.

It's a funny name. The business is still called Green Bay–Palanpur Blue. Dad, I know, named it after here—named it after Green Bay, Wisconsin.

I don't know. Crazy. Where does love come from? My father, war refugee, boy hero, Jewish diamond trader—he lived and died for the Green Bay Packers.

They were terrible when I was a kid. Do you remember the Packers in the seventies? A team God left behind, which I'm sure appealed to Dad. Even if God had forsaken the team, Wisconsin fans never stopped cheering. Dad loved Green Bay, never missed a game on TV. We watched together every week. He rarely said a word otherwise, but on game days he'd shout and jump off the couch: "You can score every time on these schlumps, Dickey!" Lynn Dickey was the quarterback then.

Dad was a cheesehead.

Here I am in Green Bay. No coincidence. Go Packers.

I didn't go to the firm alone. Julia was with me.

They were very nice. Warm. You know Indian warmth?

Yes, Indians from India. That's the second time you've asked. Do you think there are a bunch of Native Americans in the international diamond business?

Fair enough. I've heard the Oneida casino here is pretty rich.

I met the president. The firm is headed up by Bharat Jhavari, who is about my age. He's the son of Mr. Jhavari, who started the business with Dad in 1980. Bharat took us into the boardroom. He asked me to sit down, asked if I wanted something to drink. He wouldn't even look at Julia—she thought because she's a woman. I thought it might have something to do with her husband suing the firm. He was nice. He said they were so sorry about Dad. It was so sudden. Dad was family to them. How it must have been a shock to me, too. "You have no idea," I said.

Bharat wanted to make sure the lawyers had taken care of me, gotten me the money. Of course, I got the money, but not from lawyers, it didn't seem. He said he'd bought Dad out last spring. It was a terrible shock . . . Bharat shook his head. And then I got really upset about Dad, again. Dad was family to these Indians, the Jhavaris, you know? But to me . . . ? And I—I had the story of his train attack . . . And I had pictures from Antwerp. Dad in front of the train station. Dad, a young kid, at the zoo looking straight in the camera, level stare, sad. Scrawled notes to me apologizing for his absence in my life . . . notes on scraps of paper

that came in the package. My stomach clenched up and I said . . .
"Yes. Yes. It's been a terrible shock."

We didn't stay for long. Talked a little about the history . . . how
Dad met Bharat's dad in Chicago in the late seventies. How they
got the idea to export the diamond cutting to India to lower costs
instead of using the Jewish cutters. That's apparently what upset
the community so much—although that's not exactly giving
Jews over to the Nazis, is it? It was a really good partnership.
And when Dad died in June, Bharat's father came back from
India and spread the remains on a field outside of Mechelen.

No. Jews don't normally get cremated.

Bharat said he wished we could have met under better
circumstances, and he seemed sincere. Of course he was
withholding something. Not everything. Just that one thing,
Poland . . . which I guess is big.

I wouldn't have found out, Barry, except for the Jhavari bride.
She worked there, and she was Bharat's wife. Julia and I were
already at the elevator, on our way out, when she tapped me on
the shoulder. A very young woman. She had a framed picture in
her hand. "This is from last year," she said. "Your father dancing
with me at my wedding. Please have it." She handed it to me,
and there was Dad, elderly but healthy looking, energetic
looking, tuxedoed, dancing with a beautiful Indian girl. There
was Dad laughing. "Please," the Jhavari bride said. "I very much
liked your father."

Yes, this Jhavari bride, maybe twelve hours later, gave me the information. She caught me just in time. I was about to leave.

I hadn't had a single dream since entering the nursing home, not until that night.

Letter 49
Note: Copy of letter left at Hotel
Cammerpoorte front desk. N.K. verified.
October 21, 2004

Dear Cranberry,

It's just after midnight and I'm moving.

I used to think of you as my Sancho Panza. You've got your own story now. My story is done. I've found what I came for and it's time to retire.

You'll find ten thousand euros enclosed. Don't spend it all on expensive dinners.

You're an inspiration. You've grown up in two months.

Take care of yourself (and treat Kaatje like a queen—I know, you do that naturally).

I think of you as my son, Nick Kelly.

T.

Dear Julia,

I have this dream that I've told no one about. It's a recurring dream, but it sort of evolves. I believe you might be in it, except you're a tiny girl. In it, you and I are linked together so closely that we can never be separated. Sometimes you seem angry with me, and other times you protect me. I've just woken up from it now, and it's the middle of the night.

I'm leaving. I have what I need and can't stay here. I will not destabilize you.

Thank you so much, Julia. You are perfect. When I saw you in Dublin all those years ago, I knew you were amazing, someone so important to me. Who knew we'd see each other again? I'm so sorry my leaving then gave you such heartache. Who knew you'd give me this gift? You've given me my family history. Thank you. And I have no way of repaying you, except by leaving and letting you live a beautiful life.

You're pregnant. I dreamt that, too. My dreams all come true, though not all of them should. This one should. I'm so pleased, Julia.

You are lovely and bathe in light wherever you walk.

Please give hugs to Cranberry and Kaatje and your good husband, Mendez.

T.

Section III
Poland

Day Ten:
Transcript 1

Good morning.

I'm thirty-six. It's my thirty-sixth birthday.

Oh, drop it. I don't give a shit about birthdays.

Sorry, Barry. I'm joking. Happy Birthday to me.

I slept pretty well.

Poland? Are we there already?

No. I didn't just go on a whim.

Two days earlier, I'd moved over to the hotel from Julia's, because I didn't want to outstay my welcome. I was in the same hotel as Cranberry and Kaatje. Remember, it was pretty close to the train station. It was probably one a.m., and I decided to leave. Not to Poland. I thought I'd hop the first train in any direction and disappear. That's all . . . get out of Julia's hair, go do something with this new hold on my life. Then a knock on the door.

Letter 51
October 23, 2004

Dear Dad who is dead,

Are you dead? Are you?

I've crossed into Poland. I'm coming. You probably aren't surprised.

I just fell asleep on the train. Here is my dream.

A sunset light in a room . . . living room or parlor. I am in a rocking chair in a little house with my family. I know there are flowers in flower boxes in front of my windows, a pretty tree in back. And there is perfect quiet, except for the sound of my children putting together a puzzle on the floor, on the rug. A little laughing from them. And my wife is wiping the table. I am reading a book in the rocking chair above where the children play. There is so much quiet. But then comes far-off thunder. It grows. Then deeper thunder, still far away, but powerful enough to shake floorboards, to vibrate cups in the cupboard. My children look up at me. I shrug. It gets closer, closer, and I know it can't be thunder. These are explosions, punctuated explosions, with a continuous noise rolling underneath. What is that noise? I recognize the noise. It is the rumbling of tank tracks on pavement. Heavy machinery. Troops marching. The sound of those horrible engines. My children leap up to me, terrified. Nestle into me. "What's that noise?" Put their hands over their ears, little bodies shaking. They cry for protection. I don't know what to do. I am just a person and just as easily obliterated as they are. I am useless. I am desperate. My wife is Mary and the children are my children but younger than they are now and we're frozen together. It's coming and there's nothing we can do.

But then a little girl who is not my child, but is for some reason in the room with us, motions for us to follow her, takes us

---

to a cellar in back. I recognize her. She opens the door and we climb in, but she doesn't come with us. She shuts the door above us and we are together in the dark cellar.

Above us, we hear soldiers, boot stomps, crushing the material of our house, firing guns into walls—exploding plaster, the boards shaking—pushing bayonets into feather beds—sssslip—hoping to see blood, we know, they want to see our blood from the mattresses. And the children whimper, swallow sobs, and Mary can't breathe and I'm trying to keep them quiet. Please, quiet. But my children cry for protection. All that saves us is the noise of the soldiers' brutality. They destroy everything above us and I can only assume they get the little girl, too, destroy her, too. Firing, explosions, crushing glass and wood. It goes on and on until my children, exhausted by their fear, are asleep in my arms. Hours pass and there is quiet above, too.

I slowly reach up, push open the cellar door, terrified the soldiers are silent and waiting in the house. But there is no one. No house. Nothing. Glowing embers and black night sky with dim stars. There is nothing left and no sign of the little girl, but my family is alive at night in the Polish countryside.

This is how I sleep: for ten minutes, which feels like hours, waking up exhausted like I've lived a whole other, horrible life.

How are you, Dad?

I'm on my way.

T.

Day Ten:
Transcript 2

So there was this knock on the door in the middle of the night at the hotel in Antwerp. I was packing to leave. It was a messenger from the Jhavari bride, Bharat's wife. He made me follow him through the dark to a house about ten blocks away. And there she was, the Jhavari, nervous to get me information and get me away, because Bharat was asleep upstairs. And . . . in the corner . . . there was the Lady and the Unicorn tapestry chair. I almost shouted. I said, "Where did you get that?" She shushed me. She told me it was Dad's. She loved it and took it when Dad left. Left? She told me my grandmother had it in her house when Dad was a kid. The goddamn chair that the little girl sits on in my dreams . . . I thought it was Chelsea in thread . . . I couldn't let it go, but the Jhavari bride started hissing, telling me she didn't need to help me.

She gave me an address in Warsaw and said I had to inquire there. "Green Bay–Palanpur Blue sends money to that address every month," she said. "It's somehow in relation to your father." That's all she said. She told me to get out, and she meant it. I left.

Immediately. I was at the train station within an hour (I was already packed). I went to Berlin and then east.

This is when I really got sick. I felt better after the nursing home, at least in my head, no dreams . . . but with the news and being up all night and the travel . . . I couldn't breathe very well.

Huge chest congestion—I found out it was pneumonia months later. And weirdly, I guess, my eyes were dilated . . . my heart was pounding too hard, which I guess dilated my eyes . . . I bought these fat, I don't know, Jim Morrison sunglasses in Berlin. They were enormous, cartoonish. I stayed one day in Berlin, but barely left the hotel. They were the darkest, biggest sunglasses I could find. There was too much light.

Yes, I was an odd sight, I'm sure. At least I'd shaved regularly in Antwerp.

On the train, after Berlin's sprawl, the Varsovia (that was the name of the train) cut through fields of pine and birch and with my sunglasses, the light . . . was surreal . . . orange . . . I was shallow breathing . . . dizzy, which intensified the experience. And then we crossed into Poland. The trees disappeared and the earth flattened completely and the sun . . . I can't compare it to anything. Plains in Poland are not like plains in the States.

So sick, and I wasn't dressed right. At stops the doors would open and icy wind would blow through the carriage. I had a windbreaker on, but nothing warmer underneath than T-shirts and a white oxford (which I bought to meet Bharat Jhavari). But my heart was pounding, and there was so much heat inside me. I was really ill. Must've been feverish. I wouldn't have left my suitcase with that man otherwise. Stupid.

Okay. I hate thinking about it. It makes me feel terrible.

Letter 52
October 23, 2004, just past Poznan

Dear Lech Walesa,

Congratulations, President. Your country has come far.

Filthy train riders robbing me, then . . . what? Disappearing into thin air? The train didn't stop. Where the hell did he go? This is not how a democracy functions. There have to be rules. People have to obey these rules. If they don't obey, justice must be swift and terrifying. No wonder you couldn't get reelected.

When in Rome, Lech Walesa. I'm in Poland! And I had to take the edge off. I'm not sleeping very well, again, which is not good for me. In Poland you drink vodka.

An hour and a half ago after a bad dream that woke me up, I left my carriage in search of the dining car, hoping to find vodka. I found it. Dining was nearly empty, except for three unshaven men, who were huddled at the window talking in what I would describe as a conspiratorial fashion. They eyeballed me as I entered, also conspiratorially. So I shouted hello. And they glared and shook their heads. I shouldn't have looked at them at all.

Shouting a greeting is not a crime in Poland, is it? You marched with giant Solidarity banners! What about freedom of expression? What happened to that?

You Poles should take naps. The girl at the counter looked so tired, I considered knocking her down so she could sleep. Her mouth frowned at me. I frowned back at her. Her hair was bland and dirty, and her eyes were so dead blue, I thought she might really be dead, but she spoke something, I assumed asking me what I wanted. I said, "VODKA."

She gave me a vodka in a shot and two stale rolls, which I didn't order, but I don't give a fuck.

I sat down. One of the three conspirators from the other

booth stood and approached me. He said, "American?"

"Yes."

He said, "I buy vodka," and pointed at me.

"Okay," I nodded.

Forty-five minutes later, after three vodkas, after the two of us toasted Capitalism and Ronald Reagan and the Pope, I got up to take a piss. I asked the man to watch my suitcase. He smiled. "Of course, friend!" When I came back, he was gone and so was my suitcase, and his two friends shrugged. "No English," they said.

I shouted at the counter girl, but she just shrugged, her eyes watery. I ran and found a sleepy conductor, and he got other sleepy employees to search the whole train. One ancient milk-eyed man told a conductor he saw a man leap from the train and fly into the sky. Do Poles fly, Lech Walesa? Well, good sir, I might suggest they do, as the thief was not on the train! My bag was not on the train! I had pictures of my kids in that suitcase, and I don't have any clothes. How could you let this happen? There were 10,000 euros in that goddamn bag.

Poland has no right to behave so terribly. I am stripped clean, but for my backpack, which is attached to my body, thank goodness. Stripped clean! I am not impressed, Walesa.

Sincerely,

T. Rimberg

Day Ten:
Transcript 3

We'll get to the dead guy with my suitcase later. It's still hard for me to talk about. The idiocy of that thief.

At the train station in Warsaw I had a very difficult time filing a report, because the police did not care. Then I didn't know where I was going to stay, so I had no contact number, which did not please the police.

Oh yes. The police managed to find me later regardless.

Warsaw? Unbelievably cold. I mean bright with sun when I got there, but so so so cold.

I had my passport and wallet in my pants pocket. I had my notebooks and travel documents in my backpack. I had a windbreaker and T-shirt on, but nothing else. The oxford was in the suitcase with my other pants, my bathroom stuff, all that.

Terrible Stalinist architecture. Gray bloc buildings. Gray people against dull blue skies. Me shivering.

I felt . . . lost. There was no way I could negotiate the place. I heard no English. Brgz, Coorva, Booyerguszh. It sounded like the people had mouths filled with mashed potatoes. Nothing I could possibly understand. Plus I was dying from this cough. Well, not really dying, of course.

All I had was the address in Warsaw that the Jhavari bride had given me. No map. She wasn't sure exactly what the address was for. She knew cash was being sent to this address on a regular basis, that's all. I walked for three hours hoping to run into the right street. I walked and walked and walked, slower and slower, shivering, until I was an empty ache.

Nothing helpful. The doctor in Antwerp had given me strategies for handling hard times, which I'd tried to memorize, but all I could remember was *love is an action*. So I kept repeating it. Over and over again. That's a good sign you're totally losing it. The frozen air is killing you and you're walking around repeating "Love is an action," rather than looking for a warm coat.

I suppose I was telling myself I must really love my damn father to be in Poland walking around dying when I could be at home watching TV.

I did. And there are far worse places to stumble into than Le Meridien. It was getting dark when I bumped into a doorman. The doorman said, "Nice sunglasses." He was English. I was wearing my crazy shades. I'd forgotten about them. I asked him if Le Meridien was a hotel, and he laughed at me. I stayed there for a week or so, until I was arrested.

Letter 53
October 26, 2004

Dear Lech Walesa,

I have done nothing but sleep for three days. But I'm here. I don't feel well. This could be the end. But I am here, President.

What is this address? The street address the Jhavari gave me is not familiar to the staff at Le Meridien. You probably couldn't help me. You're from the famous shipyards of Gdansk.

Poland is a terrible place, Lech. I'm sorry to tell you, but you really should know.

When I sleep, I don't sleep soundly and I am washed over by energies of this place. I am told by a smiling boy at the front desk that Warsaw was leveled by Hitler. No building left standing. I could tell you this from my dreams where I am dead, a ghost, floating above the burning city. There is rubble, smoke, the little girl in black and white standing over rubble, with skinned knees, malnourished, dying. And I read about the Warsaw Ghetto. A brick wall blocking a street, blocking off a whole neighborhood. Everyone inside, dead. I've dreamt them dying. What a lovely energy comes from these streets.

I understand. I empathize. I have solidarity with the dead, Lech Walesa.

The smiling workers at the desk in the hotel squint at the address from the Jhavari, hold it up to the light, pull off their glasses, and squint again. They can't read the writing, or if they think they can, they don't recognize the street. "Maybe in Praga," one smiles. Praga is not Prague, but is a part of Warsaw across the river from here, apparently. Have you been there?

Okay, hero of the revolution. Okay, Chairman Lech. You didn't let jail time bring you down. You didn't let getting fired bring you down. You climbed the fence and led the strike. You acted. And for better or worse, you toppled Communism in this country. Heroes act. We won the cold war! I'm cold, Lech Walesa.

But love is an action. I'm going to Praga even though I cannot breathe.

Solidarity, etc.

T.

Still suicidal? In Warsaw or now?

What is suicide? Really? Everybody is dying, you know? It isn't something different than living.

Yes. I am quite deep.

I didn't even think about it in Warsaw. I mean, is this suicide? Allowing myself to fall apart? Entropy. You're falling apart right now, Barry. What are you going to do about it?

Physically you're falling apart . . . that's what life is: you reach physical maturity, then slowly die.

Okay, I can see that. You mean emotionally, spiritually.

Then I wasn't committing suicide. I was growing too. Growing while dying. Big fat growth.

Let's stick with Warsaw.

I wasn't suicidal.

When I gathered enough energy, the doorman told me how to get to Praga. And I got a map and . . . over there . . . in Praga . . . on a small street behind rail lines and warehouses, I found it. I was very surprised to find that it was a kosher butcher shop. This was the address listed on the piece of paper. My father the butcher?

I don't know why there's a kosher butcher in Warsaw. I thought, what's his market? Who buys from this guy? The shop was covered with graffiti on the outside. Skinhead Nazi graffiti. I couldn't understand the writing. But the pictures of hangman's gallows with the Star of David dangling and the swastikas spray-painted black onto the windows . . . I got it.

Correct. Not my father, at least. An enormous bearded Jewish guy with huge, big hands and an enormous head. He told me he had never heard of my father.

"No. No Rimberg." He was wrapping roasts, blood all down the front of his apron. He looked like the narrator in the *Fiddler on the Roof* movie only covered in blood. "No," he told me. "Are you going to buy meat or make questions?" I left. He intimidated me. All that blood. But out on the street, I realized I was an idiot and a weakling, so I turned around.

The bloody butcher rolled his eyes at me when I reentered. He'd moved from wrapping and was cutting long strips of muscle from backbones.

No. He didn't say anything. He kept cutting. I announced I had one more question to ask. He kept cutting. I asked the butcher if he ever got a letter or package or anything from Antwerp, from a company called Green Bay–Palanpur Blue. The butcher stopped cutting, squinted at me. "Not from company. But from Antwerp." He pronounced a name, something like Shaj bar-e. I wrote Jhavari on a piece of butcher paper, and he got red in the face, real nervous. "I do service. Take some money, hold envelope until woman from bookstore come to pick up. Each month bill Shaj bar-e Antwerp for kosher meat." I then convinced the butcher I was going to arrest him if he didn't give up the name of the bookstore. "You are in serious trouble with the United Nations," I told him. I said the money was meant to fund terrorists and he was a dupe, funneling cash to Islamic terrorists.

Indeed, my friend. Very dramatic.

Yes. He gave me good information. I found the bookstore. Watanabe Bookstore.

It was the most amazing thing I've ever experienced.

Right. But I told you, I don't remember the accident.

Cover Letter,
faxed to Fr. Barry McGinn,
August 19, 2005

Dear Father McGinn,

   Attached you will find three message from T. Rimberg. He contacted me via these notations, by leaving with cashier at bookstore I own with my husband. I had only learned of T. existence and also his brother in June 2004, when my father arrived to Warsaw to live. I am most happy to assist your investigations as I am able. T. departed Warsaw in May with boy with blue hair (Nik) and I have not heard of him in several weeks and become very concerned. It is happy news he is safe. My mother will be very pleased to know this.

   Regards,

   Paulina Watanabe

Note 1,
Faxed to Fr. Barry McGinn,
August 19, 2005

October 27, 2005

Dear Ms. Watanabe,

I am trying to locate one Josef Rimberg. I have shaken down the kosher butcher and gathered information that leads me to believe you are in direct contact with him, or at least might provide specific clues regarding his whereabouts. I am from a special investigative branch of the United Nations and I will have you arrested and jailed if you do not contact me immediately. You, Ms. Watanabe, have run afoul of international laws re: laundering money for terroristic purposes. I am at Le Meridien.

Sincerely,

T. Rimberg
United Nations—New York
Financial Investigations

Day Ten:
Transcript 5

Well, I might have been ashamed, if I hadn't been in the middle
of dying from pneumonia.

Yes, I used my own name. It was a tip-off. T. Rimberg looking
for Josef Rimberg. I don't suppose a secret agent would scrawl an
official communication on hotel stationery, either.

I received one reply by the next morning. It just said something
like "Father dead. Leave us be."

I didn't believe Dad was dead. I'd heard that before. I believed
Dad wanted me to be in Poland. I believed he was waiting for
me. I left the hotel to get a coat at an outdoor flea market
because I was freezing and figured I'd have to walk around a lot
to . . . do surveillance.

Yes, it's the black fur coat from the picture. Full-length sable. I
looked crazy. And with those shades? I looked like P. Diddy.
That coat probably saved my life, though. I needed warmth. Poor
little sables died so I might live.

Paulina left two more messages at Le Meridien while I was out.

She said she knew who I was and she wouldn't be shaken down. The second one said that I should meet her and her mother at the store at five p.m.

She thought I knew who she was, which I didn't. She thought I knew about Dad. I didn't. I also didn't have a clue why she would bring her mother. Didn't really care. I was so ill, Barry. I just wanted to see Dad and tell him I loved him before I died. Love as an action.

I received the messages at two p.m. when I returned from the market. Then slept until 5:15. I got to the store forty-five minutes late, and there she was.

Letter 54
October 28, 2004

Dear Hayley Mills,

I'm drunk from my secret sister's vodka.

You know that scene in *Parent Trap* when you're in the green nether world of summer camp and you realize that the girl you hate with the short bob who looks like you (who is also played by you in the film) is actually your twin sister separated at birth? She's got her mother's picture and that picture is also of your mother? And then she (the other, bob-haired you) cries on your camp bunk and you comfort and hug her (you)?

I know how you feel, except there is no hope.

I've been separated from my half-sister Paulina by circumstances and geography and culture, too, and so I didn't know she existed, and then I dreamt her for two months, except she was tinier in my dreams than now. And then there was a lightning storm inside her bookstore, and I wanted to beat Paulina because I was so terrified (like you fighting yourself at the camp dance when you and your sister, whom you didn't know was your sister yet, are bitter rivals). I also wanted to pull out my hair. Paulina doesn't look like me but looks like my brother David if he weren't fat and old.

And I'll tell you this, Hayley Mills: No matching bobbed haircuts can put us back together. There's no one left to trap. There are no ranches in California, no mansions in Boston, no crafty double-crossing plans to make us whole. This is Poland, Hayley Mills. Godforsaken Poland. My stepmother is a fat Polish woman named Jadwiga who doesn't say a word, but is puckered and concerned and crying. Everyone dies in Poland, Hayley.

I have twin daughters who remind me of you. Little, blond pipsqueaks with sharp tongues. I think there was a remake of your movie, because my daughters exchanged places last summer to confuse me when I was drunk. You make me so sad, Hayley Mills. But we have so much in common.

Are you alive? My father isn't.

I have a sister in Poland.

T. Rimberg

Day Ten,
Transcript 6

When I walked in the door and we met eyes, it was like standing in the middle of an explosion that wouldn't stop. Blinding light, and the room spun, and our eyes were locked, and the light crashed around us . . . audibly and it . . . echoed. And then Paulina started screaming bloody terror, and the books shook and windows rattled, and I cried out, "It's you . . . It's you . . . It's you . . ." And then coughing took me down, coughing and coughing that doubled me over. I had to brace myself, hold myself up against a stack. And Paulina shouted, screamed in Polish.

I had no idea yet she was my sister.

No. Not Julia. Paulina, without question, without doubt. Paulina was the little girl in my dreams.

The two of us could barely talk—we were both shaken. I mean, Jesus Christ, Barry. She said, "I dream you every night."

Yes, same dreams. Or similar. I mean, hers seemed to have her acting and me showing up in them . . . so not exactly my dreams . . . but war dreams. And sometimes I'd save her. Sometimes I'd laugh at her and run away and she'd be destroyed.

Oh, but she did say she dreamed getting attacked by old ladies right around the time I was in Antwerp.

We dreamed more . . . together . . . after we were actually together.

Poor Pani Jadwiga, Paulina's mother, had no idea what was going on. She stood there with her mouth open. I mean, Pani Jadwiga knew Dad, the father of her daughter, had kids from another marriage—apparently he'd talked about me often. But this thing between Paulina and me . . . how do you explain that?

Paulina pulled a bottle of vodka from under the register, and we drank and stared at each other, and Pani mumbled at us in Polish and shook her head. I couldn't have explained it to Pani even if I thought she knew English. She did know English, by the way.

I gathered enough information to understand that this old woman was my father's romantic partner and that this dream person—this Paulina was my sister.

Yes. I've identified my grandmother Aida in photographs since then. David and Paulina look like Aida. All dark hair and dark eyes.

We got bombed. I was so ill I couldn't stand. Paulina put me in a car that took me back to my hotel. We agreed to meet the next day. I laughed hysterically all the way to the hotel. I think I was in shock. The driver mumbled at me in Polish and shook his head. I said to him "Pani Jadwiga!"

I was arrested, which is what kept me in Poland. So no, we didn't meet the next day.

October 29, 2004

I hope you are well, sister. I received your message about meeting together an hour later than we'd planned this afternoon. But I cannot. In a moment I will go with the police. I am being questioned about the death of a man who stole my suitcase on the train from Berlin. I did not kill this man. I assume he jumped, but the serving girl in the dining carriage is certain she remembers me throwing this man from the train. I'm sorry to miss our appointment. I'll be in contact soon.

T.

Note 3,
Faxed to Fr. Barry McGinn,
August 19, 2005

October 29, 2004

Dear sister,

I write to tell you I am the prime suspect in the murder of
Pawel Kowolski. He is dead, having fallen from a speeding train
with my personal belongings in his hands. There are three
witnesses who claim they saw me lift Pawel above my head and
throw him out the window. Two were his friends in the dining
car who pretended they didn't know where he was after he
disappeared. The other was the attendant in the dining car who
looked to be strung out on some barbiturate. Do you know of a
lawyer? I asked the investigator, who has a crew cut, why the
three witnesses did nothing to prevent my murderous act and
did nothing to stop the train after Pawel flew from it. He said I
have no right to make such questions with him. I make such
questions because I was in the bathroom when Pawel stole my
suitcase and I don't want to be in jail. In any case, I am not
guilty and am dying of a cough. Could you please help me in
some way? I am in lock-up at the police headquarters (komenda
glowna—is that right?), where I am periodically asked ridiculous
questions. I hope this gets to you. I don't have your phone and
am depending on the smiling hotel concierge to get you this
message.

T.

Day Ten:
Transcript 7

Yes, finally in jail. Where I belonged. It had been a long time coming.

No, I don't mean that at all. I wasn't even philosophical about it. In Paris, if someone accused me of killing someone, I would've said, "Yes. That's me. I murder just like everyone else. Put me away." In Antwerp I would likely have thought, "I'm crazy. Oh no. I did it and don't remember." But I remembered exactly what happened on the train.

I wasn't in jail for long—a lot longer than I should've been. I was never charged. Spent a couple of days trapped in there.

Oh yeah. Serious jail. They put me in a cell.

The crew cut man kept telling me, "Not arrested." Bullshit.

So damn sick! I was feverish and kept passing out. There was a wet cot in the cell they stuck me in. Bad sleep.

Yes, I do. I'll probably always feel guilty about the Polish man, even though I know I didn't throw him from the train. He'd likely be alive right now if I hadn't ventured aboard the Varsovia on that particular day. It's strange to think of our crossed destinies . . . the fact that I was born and quit my job and left for Europe was part of his. Part of his destiny was my affair with Chelsea. But I had no intent and wouldn't have harmed him. Maybe he would've jumped off the train that day with someone else's bag. Who knows? He didn't have a very good escape plan.

The Polish authorities took my backpack for a chunk of time at one point, which made me go ballistic—I screamed all kinds of profanity at them, which didn't help my cause. I don't know what they read or what they got out of it, but when they returned my notebooks they'd pulled all the metal spirals out of them and my pack was filled with loose paper.

Maybe they read the suicide letters and thought I'd kill myself with the wire?

Of course I asked.

The crew cut guy spoke reasonable English, but he wouldn't tell me why. He kind of "pff'd" when I asked what the hell, and curled his lip and shook his head.

Pani Jadwiga. She stitched them back together with yarn. She's very sweet. She knows how important documents of this type are to Rimbergs.

I didn't belong in jail. But Paulina and Pani Jadwiga took their time getting me out. Even when they did get me out, they didn't tell me I'd been cleared.

Oh no. No. No. I don't blame them. I love these women. I love my sister as myself. Poor sister! I missed her twenty-fifth birthday last month. She was born eleven months after Dad left me.

Is that a pizza guy at the door?

Dear Kara and Sylvie,

Happy Birthday! Happy Birthday! Happy Birthday!

I have ten-year-old girls! I remember the day you were born.
Me and your mother were so amazed at this gift. Not one, but
two beautiful and healthy daughters. Your mother always told
me to expect twins. Aunt Carol had twins. But I couldn't believe
it, even when we saw you both on the ultrasound. Two girls?
Could I be so lucky? When you were born, I hugged you both in
my arms and promised you I would give you everything. I
cried—I was so happy and exhausted. When Charlie was born,
your mother and I would fight over who got to hold him. When
you two came, we each got a beautiful girl to hug and whisper
to. If I could live the day of your births over and over and never
leave that day, I would be the happiest man on the planet.

When you turn twenty-five, think how young you feel, then
think of me at that same age, witnessing the birth of twin
daughters. It was perfection.

Happy Happy Birthday!

I love you.

Dad

Letter 56
Written from police headquarters,
Warsaw, Poland
October 31, 2004

Hello Charlie, my boy,

It's Halloween. Are you going trick-or-treating? You're almost twelve, just a few days until your birthday. You're not too old to go door-to-door, yet, are you? What are you going to be? I bought the funniest-looking sunglasses you've ever seen. I wish I were at home with you, so you could use them. I can imagine all the poses you'd strike wearing these shades. It just makes me laugh. My dramatic, beautiful boy.

I love you, Charlie.

Dad

Day Eleven:
Transcript 1

Thanks for the birthday pizza last night. I'd nearly forgotten what good food tastes like.

Yes. I finally saw it on the *Today* show. Aren't all those people hampering the clean-up?

The lights were blurry on the videotape they showed. I couldn't really tell.

Have you been out there?

What do you think, Barry?

I'd like to see it, I think.

NBC makes me look pretty. Mary (my ex-wife, not the virgin) must have given them the picture. It was taken during Charlie's first birthday party. It's my favorite.

I was young, about Paulina's age.

What do you know about All Souls' Day, Barry?

Yes, huge in Poland.

That's how I left jail, the excuse Paulina gave them—or at least told me she gave them. She said I was dying (which seemed true) and I was in Poland to visit the graves of loved ones on All Souls' Day and I would be returned to the jail by my family.

I never went back to jail. It was a lie, actually. Paulina knew the druggie train attendant in the dining cart had retracted her statement about me killing Pawel.

I didn't find out I was off the hook until the embassy tracked me down in the spring. That's right about the time Cranberry showed up, too.

Paulina was pissed. She and Pani Jadwiga had to pay a lot of money to get me untangled from the legal system over there, even though I was innocent. Corruption, you know? They had to bribe some commissioner to get me out quickly. Paulina said it was an ass-load of money . . . And, you know, Paulina had only met me that one time . . . we hadn't even talked yet, more than cursorily, about the dreams . . . although she dreamed about the jail cell I was in and Brett Favre, too. She didn't know me like she does now. They'd paid lots and lots of money to get Dad cancer treatments, too, and they really were dependent on the money coming from the Jhavaris month-to-month. I'd upset the kosher butcher with my threats, so that relationship was endangered.

That's what I'm saying. Paulina was brutal and stayed that way a lot with me the first month or so. When she was really drunk, she'd threaten to hand me back to the authorities, which scared me, because I didn't know I was free. And I was sick and weak and I didn't want to leave Pani Jadwiga—she's the sweetest stepmom a guy could have.

Am I angry? At Paulina?

Paulina needed me. She needed to keep me in Warsaw. She was mad as hell, but she needed me. I'm not angry at all.

Paulina is lonely. She still needs me.

You know?

On the phone?

I am her family. Other than her mom, I'm it.

Barry . . . it seems like your investigation . . . it seems like you're gathering more information than what's really pertinent to . . .

Do you really find that proof in this story?

I feel very fortunate to have met you, Barry. You are a very nice human being.

I'm okay. I'm okay.

I would like to take a break.

Journal Entries,
November 3–5

It is a concrete smokestack on the outside. Concrete blocks, but inside the floors are wood and covered in Persian rugs. Still, it is spooky. Cold. You are sleeping in the bedroom where your father slept. There's still an IV drip in the corner.

Liver cancer.

Pani Jadwiga and Paulina share a room in this mausoleum.

God, she is hateful. Wakes you up by throwing a shoebox on your chest. "Wake up, sleepy," she says after the box hits you. You've slept for two days. The cough is deep. Dirty French river water in your lungs. She's been waiting for Pani Jadwiga to leave so she can attack you. Now she throws a box on your sick chest. Nice sister.

You look in the box. Are you dreaming? He wrote, "Spit out of a river, nothing. I've been shot and my brothers torn to pieces." Who was spit out of a river?

The man was obsessed. There are hundreds of letters and notes and scraps covered in writing. Crazy man wrote to Brett Favre dozens of times. What old European Jewish man writes to a quarterback? Crazy father. "Interceptions are nothing. They just show you live on that tightrope!" Crazy man.

There is a note to Charlie. Dad tells him to say yes.

You make a big show of how your father was crazy. Pani Jadwiga eyeballs you from her chair, while she cuts a picture of a bird out of the newspaper. "He wrote letters to football players!" You shake your head.

"I look in your packet," says Paulina.

"What packet?" you ask.

"For your back," says Paulina.

"You read my notebooks?" you shout.

"You write suicide letter to Madonna. Tell me about crazy father."

Okay.

Letter 57
November 5, 2004

Dear Brett Favre,

I am not the kind of guy who travels halfway around the world to find his father alive.

A couple of days ago, Mr. Favre, I was lying on a cot in a cold Polish jail cell where I hadn't slept for three days, because of coughing. Without sleeping, I began to hallucinate. Often, I'd hallucinate you throwing footballs and me and my sister watching from the sidelines cheering. That's ridiculous.

I was dreaming of you when I heard the cell door open. I was dreaming of you when an animal attacked me, except it wasn't an animal, it was my sable coat, which was thrown on top of me by a guard. I didn't struggle under the weight of the coat. I figured my number was up and the animal could eat me and I'd die. But then my angry sister entered the jail cell and without saying hello pulled me to standing and helped me put on the sable coat. Then she grabbed my backpack and she walked me out of the jail. Nobody said goodbye. Nobody answered my question, which was: "What is going on?"

My sister, Paulina, walked me to her car, this odd-looking French car with a faded orange paint job. She stuck me in the backseat, threw my backpack on top of me, and drove to a flower shop. While she was in the flower shop, the sun was bright and I found my Jim Morrison shades, which had gotten bent, in my coat pocket. I put them on. I was still half asleep, blurry, dizzy, and I heard voices. A gang of kids surrounded the car. They pressed their faces to the windows and shouted at me in Polish, which is a horrible language. Then Paulina returned carrying bags and bags of noxious flowers. She yelled at the kids, which made them scatter. She opened the squeaky car door and threw the flowers on me. Inside the car she said, "These childrens should be at cemetery. Not harassing infirm American."

Exactly what I was thinking, Mr. Favre. Why would kids want to hang out at a cemetery?

We drove out of the city and I had to go to the bathroom, which made Paulina glare. We stopped at a bar with chicken wire on the walls, which apparently was hung there to keep plaster from falling all over the floor. Men in the bar shouted at me, because I looked funny. Paulina shouted at the men and they fell silent.

Back in the car, we continued to drive. I asked where. Paulina said nothing.

The sun was setting, the sky coloring orange, darkening the orange of the car. We drove down a road lined with tall birch trees and into a line of cars that moved slowly. We ended up at a cemetery and parked just outside it with hundreds of other cars. There was a line of cars stretching as far as I could see behind us. We parked. And I asked, "Is this Dad's funeral?" Paulina shook her head, no.

I knew my father was dead.

Paulina climbed out. She carried candles she'd had on the front seat, and instructed me to carry the bags of flowers. I did and followed her into the cemetery as the sky was getting dark. I took off my shades and saw we were surrounded by tall trees, orange sky decaying into streaks of blue and purple, the sun coloring everything, as it went down. We crunched over dead leaves, the smell of their decay thick in the air. We waded through crowds of people surrounding graves covered in flowers and lit candles, which made pools of light. People whispered; there were no loud voices, like a mass funeral for everybody.

We came to the family plot. Mitsunori Watanabe, my sister Paulina's husband, was one grave. She put down some candles around Mitsunori's grave. She lit them. Then she took the flowers from my arms and arranged them delicately around the candles. Then she started to sob and then she fell over onto the ground.

I stood there.

The Polish are obsessed with the dead, Mr. Favre. Instead of harassing infirm Americans, most of them spend November 1 at the cemetery.

For Paulina, it's easy to remember—her memories haven't faded, because her husband died only six months ago. She and Mitsunori were both biologists. They met in the mountains on the Czech border. Paulina, still a student, was on vacation and was hiking, and Mitsunori, a Japanese mountain climber, was traveling. They fell in love. Mitsunori moved to Warsaw and opened a bookstore. Last spring, for their second anniversary, they went to Indonesia to do some kind of ecotourism in the pristine rainforests. Mitsunori was shot by thieves in their rental car. He died on Paulina's lap. That's all I know. I've known my sister for less than ten days.

Mr. Favre, I watched Paulina while she sobbed, then I couldn't take it—my chest ached, too, from the dirty water I'd inhaled in Paris and also from sadness for my sister. Then I looked up and saw Pani Jadwiga, Paulina's mother, my dad's partner for twenty-five years, and she was standing there surrounded by the depleting fall light, and she was crying real softly, I knew, for my dad. I walked to her and asked her where Dad's grave was. She hugged me and said, "No grave."

My dad died on August 23 of this year, about eight months after your dad died. My dad had liver cancer, so it took him a while to go. Nothing shocking like the sudden heart attack your dad had. Except I didn't know my dad was sick until I found out that he's dead—I've come all the way from Minnesota to see him.

The last night I was fully part of my own family, fully with my wife and kids, was the night after your dad died, when you played that Monday night football game against the Raiders. Me and Mary (my wife, who would start divorce proceedings against me a few weeks later) let our kids stay up to watch. You were so amazing, Mr. Favre, throwing four touchdown passes in the first half, flinging the ball between defenders, completing everything. It did seem like your dad was up there in the heavens guiding all your throws to perfection. It was incredible, Mr. Favre. At half-time, Mary and I cried and hugged, because everything we believed about ourselves was turning out false and your dad had died and you were so raw and emotional and perfect.

Christmas was a few days later and I behaved horribly and that sealed my family's fate.

So just a few days ago, on November 1, I found myself sitting cross-legged on the ground in this Polish cemetery, back against a birch tree, watching my sister Paulina crying on the ground in front of her husband's gravestone. I watched her mother, Pani Jadwiga, my father's lover, bend over her to rub her back while whispering to her. I found myself thinking of you. And inexplicably, the whole scene filled with light.

My father loved you, Brett. He was your biggest fan (although I didn't know that yet when I sat in the cemetery). And just like me, he was not a good communicator except on paper—letter after letter he wrote, to you and everybody else, by far the lion's share of which he never sent. I don't send letters, either. But I'm writing you a letter to tell you my dad loved your interceptions as much as your touchdown passes. He loved that you take such great joy in doing what you do best. I'm communicating for him, even though he's gone.

With much respect,

T. Rimberg

Day Eleven:
Transcript 2

I didn't know Brett Favre's life had gotten so traumatic again last year.

You know, I was in the home in Antwerp when his brother-in-law died, and I was dying in Poland when his wife was diagnosed with breast cancer. I figured that out later, back in June, when I was at Motel 6 in Milwaukee with all that time on my hands.

Dad scribbled on everything. He had scraps and scraps of paper filled with tiny words in this boot-sized shoebox. More writing than I've ever done.

Same kinds of things I found in the inheritance envelope I got in Minneapolis. Odd pictures with writing all over the back. Napkins, receipts, newspapers with marker writing over the top. Lots I couldn't read at all.

Yes, I know. I am my father's son.

Most in English, yeah. He learned it early and was in the U.S. by the time he was fourteen, so he communicated in English.

I am far more organized with my writing. Especially after Pani

Jadwiga put my notebooks back together.

Dad had been expecting me. Paulina told me when we were leaving the cemetery.

Right. He died August 23. It was the sixtieth anniversary of the last gassings at Auschwitz.

He went into a coma on August 19, my thirty-fifth birthday, the day both I and Paulina first dreamt of each other.

No. Not there. Dad certainly wasn't in the cemetery.

Do you really want to know?

He was cremated. He's out on the interstate where I hit that bus.

Journal Entries,
November 6–9

In the middle of a dream of Chelsea's living room. You are making love. Then Dad taps your shoulder. You turn to look at him. He's orange. He stands over you, slaps your face. "So that is your action? That is your love? You schtup your secretary and call it love?"

"She isn't my secretary," you shout at him.

"Jadwiga was my secretary," Dad says.

Behind him, Paulina as a little girl shakes her head at you.

In the morning, Paulina shouts, "You are here. Stay out of my dreams."

"I can't even get laid," you shout back.

"What is laid?" Paulina asks.

I am disgusting, you think.

Breakfast. You've just read a note to Paulina from Dad. In it he wrote, "You are not alone, my girl. You have two brothers, two nieces, and three nephews. They should know you."

Paulina sits across from you, glaring. "You have wife. He told me you have wife and left her. I read in your notebook how you treat wife."

"No," you say. "Not wife. My wife divorced me."

"And childrens? He said I am auntie. I see you write childrens."

"Stop reading my goddamn notebooks," you say.

"You are like father," she nods. "Disappeared, and no good." She nods again.

"No," you say.

"Yes," she sneers. She stands from the table, says, "Like him. You disappear."

You can almost hear the growl in the scrawled words on the paper. He and Paulina were fighting. He's angry. It's so hard to read his shaky hand.

"You think it's about what you get? You think this between us should have been a transaction? Me giving something to you? Human life isn't tit for this, tat for that. We are connected. We are for each other. We are more than our transaction. This is love, daughter. I made you. That's what I did. And what good was I to you after? I chased money. I know you think he won't come. But he will, and then you can ask Theodore what good I am to him. Better for him I'm not there. Better for him to love me as he does. Now you stop shouting at me. I'm not a well man!"

You and Paulina are alike. You and your father were alike. You are assholes.

Today you walked outside with Pani Jadwiga. She treats you like a little boy. She bought you a chocolate. Outside were tall concrete apartment blocks surrounded by gray parking lots and dirty cars and long brown grass around a dirty pond. Perfect blue sky. You imagine the Baltic. Ice cold air felt good in your lungs. There was a layer of ice across the pond. Jadwiga talked and talked in Polish. Babbled away, as if you could understand. She pointed at birds and hooted, called to them. Laughed at her own jokes. Grabbed your arm so she could hold it as you walked together. Bubbling Pani Jadwiga. Paulina will not look at you. How can her mother be so sweet?

Why are you not in jail? Why are you here? They will come. Paulina will call them and they will put you back in that jail and you will die. He is dead. His body is rotting. They never gave you back the suitcase he stole from you. There are pictures of your children. Little faces staring up from school photos, buried in a Polish trash pit. He's dead. He's dead. It's too dark in this fucking room.

Dad wrote to you, but didn't send it.

"When everything is gone, you want it back. My father. My mother. I wanted back what we had lost and I built it. But only the money. And now it's too late, Theodore, to give it to you. I don't want you to have to build back. I want you to be free of this. But you aren't here. God damn it, tell your brother I don't want to die without us talking, Theodore. Tell David. Unforgiving boy. He should forgive."

It's the only time he's addressed David. Your father sounds confused.

David will not forgive.

You, after much fretting, after thinking about what Dad wanted to give but didn't, call David at his office to tell him the news of your father's death. You have to travel with Paulina to the post office to make an international call that won't be collect.

"You're where?" David growls.

You say where.

"With Dad?"

You tell him not with Dad, because Dad is dead.

"This family is completely ridiculous. I thought you were dead. Mary thought you were dead. She called me panicking. I tracked you to Holland. I mean, the police tracked you to Holland, you missing person."

You tell him you were searching for Dad.

"Perfect. Irresponsible, loser son chases down asshole father. World is a better place, huh? Harmonic convergence."

You say again, putting emphasis on dead, that Dad is DEAD.

David says good riddance. David tells you he'll call Mary. David tells you you're not welcome to contact him again. He hangs up the phone.

You look over at Paulina, who is leaning against another bank of phones. You tell her, "David says goodbye."

This is funny. A letter to you written on an old receipt roll, purple numbers printed on the opposite side from the handwriting, like it was pulled from a cash register. Funny, or not so funny.

"You think you want to know truth? Fine. Your grandfather was attacked by a mob in Holland after he escaped Antwerp. The underground tracked him over there, where he was living as a Catholic. They worked him over, beat him, and dragged him around for two hours before they strung him up. They strung up my mother, too. That's how well he was liked. Not very much.

"Some of this I knew. I heard things after the war before your Uncle Solly brought me to the States.

"Some I found out just in 1979 when Lev Goldstein wanted to apologize to me in Chicago. Lev was part of this mob in Holland when he was sixteen. Lev, who owned some retail shop in a fancy suburb north of the city with his nice tie and jacket, helped murder my father. I know my father had it coming, but not my mother, Theodore. Not your grandmother. Lev said she wouldn't get out of the way and she kicked and scratched those guys. Lev told me he was haunted by this, the murder of my mother, and had to apologize. I broke Lev's nose in a restaurant when he told me my father died screaming curses and my mother died sobbing and screaming for my father. I was in such a state, I had too much to drink. I phoned Jadwiga and told her I needed to see her, because we'd been out to dinner many times on my trips to Chicago and she was a good secretary and I knew she loved me, despite my circumstances, and I needed her. I only came home one more time to say goodbye to you, Theodore. And here I am at the end, and I want to curse life like my father? This I don't want to give to you, my son, curses. I don't want us to curse life."

Dad ran home to Europe with Jadwiga but wouldn't live with her, even after she had his child. Not pretty.

Dreamed last night of James Lofton catching a pass on a sunny day at Lambeau Field. You and Dad and Paulina were down on the sidelines and the sun was high and the football blotted out the sun, then James Lofton jumped twenty feet in the air and pulled it down before being tackled.

At breakfast, Paulina comes late and says, "I might like tanks and Nazis more than watching these sports." She smiles, though. Sends shivers through your body.

"Football?" Pani Jadwiga asks. "Chicago Bears. Walter Payton! Nice smile."

"You do not speak English," Paulina snarls at her.

"Walter Payton is dead," you mumble.

Pani Jadwiga cries, "Oh!" She leaves the table, crying.

So much crap in this box and you can't stay awake to read it all. Some letters are not addressed, but seem to be to you. At night, Paulina paces around the apartment, and you can't sleep unless she does, but are too tired to read. And then all day you both sleep and dream of Green Bay. Tonight is Kristallnacht, Paulina informs you. You never drink with her, but agree you will drink tonight, because, apparently, Kristallnacht was important to Dad. Kristallnacht is important. November 9.

First you will finish reading these things.

One last note is glued to the back of a newspaper filled with soccer scores. You had to peel it away slowly to not damage it.

Then this.

"Theodore, I mailed you that letter. I made it plain to you that I am dying and you should come visit me here in Warsaw, but it doesn't matter what I say, because you won't come in time. I have maybe five minutes and I will be out again with this dripping medicine. I dream and I'm awake but never completely awake again. You know I know your children? I know Charlie and Sylvie and Kara. I know their names and even have had pictures of them your mother sent to me. I want to tell you that your mother invited me to come visit when Charlie was born. She invited me, but I didn't. I told her no. I told her I had too much business and you wouldn't want to see me after all this time. Don't be upset with your mother, because she tried. Even with all her depression and craziness, she tried hard for you and invited me to come meet my grandson. Now when I sleep I hear echoes of these children. I dream them, too. I dream them playing on the floor in front of me, just like I was a good grandpa, and I tell them how beautiful they are. I'm afraid that too late I realized I am like my father who put business in front of people. I always thought that I'm not like him. I used my dreams to feel close to my family and he used his to frighten people, to gain advantage. I am not like him, I said. He worked for Nazis and I set his victims free. I am not like him. But even if I was treated as some kind of hero, it was only one train, Theodore. It was only one action. I let it go to my head, that I wasn't like my father, because I risked everything to save people. But it was only one train on one day. And my good family was only a dream.

"I dream of my grandchildren and they are good kids, but time changes everything, and they might not stay good kids. You have to tell them I love them.

"Theodore, when I'm not asleep, I feel Jadwiga's hand on my head and she says, 'Nyeh, nyeh, nyeh, nyeh.' That means no over and over. I tell her to speak in English, because she can. You have to watch out what you say in front of her, because she has some big ears and she lived in Chicago two years, so she plays dumb, but she understands and she listens. She doesn't want to speak English. She only ever wants to speak French with me because English makes her feel guilty that she broke up my marriage, which she didn't. And now she says in Polish, 'No.' I tell her to stop saying no when I have the energy. I want her to say yes. But that makes no sense to her. Theodore, I want you to say yes. Do you understand what I'm telling you? You say yes to your children. You say yes to Paulina. You say yes whenever you should say yes. Paulina will have to say yes, too, even though her poor Japanese is dead. Losing someone you love is quite a shock. I know. You know it too. But I'm telling you right now, you can't say no, Theodore. You have no excuse. I want you to say yes. That's it.

"Today I don't have good dreams. Today I dream I am a stormtrooper breaking up furniture, setting fire, while a whole family of Jews cowers and cries. This is Kristallnacht in my dream. I'll tell you what, if I wasn't so sick, I would fight that dream. I would turn myself into a good guy and I would fight. I'm very sick, Theodore. Too sick, I'm afraid to say.

"So goodbye, Theodore.

Your Father"

Kristallnacht is tonight.

In the first sentence of that last gluey note, Dad says his letter is too late? The inheritance notes gave no indication he was dying, no indication where he was, no indication you should visit. Was there another letter? You ask Paulina, who is already drunk, if he means the notes you received with the inheritance back in Minneapolis. She shakes her head no. You tell her to stop saying no. She shouts, "The letter he wrote you that you don't listen to for two months!"

You say, "As God is my witness, I did not receive another letter other than what was in the inheritance envelope."

"I do not believe in God," Paulina shouts back.

You and Paulina glare at each other. You push the gluey final note into Paulina's face. She grabs it from your hand. She reads. She pauses. She says, "Yes. There is other letter. You don't know this letter? We send."

You shake your head no.

"I am sorry, Theodore," she says. "I am sorry." There is so much empathy in her eyes. She passes you the bottle. Then you begin to drink.

"To our father," you say.

"To Father," she nods.

And soon everything is slow with booze. From the bedroom Pani Jadwiga's deep snores shake. And Paulina, now sitting on the floor, says, "Brother, if you do not know last letter, why do you come to Warsaw?"

You squint at her, thoughts muddled, unsteady. You squint at your sister and say, "I don't know."

Paulina nods and smiles.

Day Twelve:
Transcript 1

Thank you. Good morning to you.

Me and Faye watched the Packer game on TV last night.

Faye is so great. Hi Faye. She'll hear this because we're recording, right?

Hi Faye!

Yeah, they got thumped . . . but preseason . . . you know, whatever. Favre looked good. He threw that touchdown.

Wow. I bet you're right. He probably does know who I am now. Weird.

I'm glad you enjoyed the game.

Well, there isn't much left to tell, Father B.

Correct. My father had written to me again, a few days before he went into a coma. He did send the letter but made the mistake of

---

addressing it himself—a banker in Switzerland had addressed the
inheritance envelope. Dad's handwriting was so bad, it took the
post office a while to figure out where to deliver it.

I was already in Europe when it arrived, otherwise I would have
gone right to Poland and would've avoided all that crazy stuff,
would've avoided Amsterdam and Paris and Julia in Antwerp.

Maybe. Maybe I'll get there, Father B. I suppose—I guess I
can't imagine who I'd be right now if I hadn't jumped in the
river or . . . broken into my father's apartment. It isn't like I'd
wish that stuff on anyone, though.

It took me a month before I realized Dad was in this crazy vase
covered with birds. Everything in Pani's room is covered with
birds. Bird photos, bird paintings, she had a bird bedspread. A
vase on her dresser covered with birds didn't catch my attention.

Sometime in December . . . Paulina was drinking. She
whispered, "Father is in a vase!" We went creeping into Pani's
room and tiptoed up to it, but Pani woke up and shouted at us.

Of course I took a closer look later. I spoke to Dad. Not literally . . .
to his remains.

I was with Paulina on that. I got drunk with her all the time.
Pani would cook for us and clean. The kosher butcher decided

he'd keep taking the business checks after Pani and Paulina took me down there and I apologized . . . so we had money. Paulina and I drank.

I haven't had a dream since November 9 of last year. Kristallnacht. Paulina stopped dreaming, too. So we communed the only way we knew how, I guess. Got into a common state of inebriation.

It really just made it easy to talk and laugh. We played cards a lot.

Sometimes. She gave me a black eye once. She's very strong.

It was messy. Sometimes we'd sleep on the floor under the dining room table. We were pretty serious about drinking.

I didn't think about anything. I just was. My health was pretty bad, you know? I didn't have a lot of energy to think about the future. Especially with all that drinking.

I grew to love Poland. I love that place. At least I grew to really love the apartment and the grounds right around it. The building felt like home. We didn't leave much, sometimes not for weeks at a time.

By spring. When it started getting warm and I wasn't getting better. All winter I believed my health would improve when it warmed up. But it warmed up and I still felt horrible. Then I got scared. I stopped drinking in spring. So did Paulina—she started running, decided to train for road races, which is a better way to . . . you know. Deal with loss.

You know how.

Yes, Cranberry, agent of change.

He took Kaatje to meet his mother, back in St. Paul. During that trip, in April, he picked up my mail from the post office. Cranberry found the letter from Dad. It led him right to Warsaw.

Poor kid thought I was dead.

Letter from Josef Rimberg mailed to T. Rimberg on August 15, 2004. Handwritten address nearly illegible. Delivered to T. in Warsaw by Nick Kelly, May 2005.

August 15, 2004

Dear Theodore, my good boy,

I'm afraid it is late. I had some big plans, but as soon as your father gets afraid to die, he starts keeling over right then.

Dying has never been a worry to me. I rode a horse right up to a train while Germans tried to kill me and never was afraid to die, not even when one of their bullets hit me on my hip. Never afraid, because what did I want to live for? My terrible father? My poor mother? I knew they would not survive the war even though my father would do everything to survive, lie, steal, kill everyone else to stay alive. I knew he would die and I would never see him again. You know what his great wish to live got him? A noose for both him and my mother in Holland. That's another story. You worry too much about beating death, you start dying. I never worried about it, but now I am.

I got cancer in my liver. The doctors told me I might have a year to live and I believed them. So I made some plans. I will tell you this, no government in Belgium is going to get my money. What did they ever do for the Jews? And then they think they should have my money? I moved some assets, made arrangements with my business partners, then I paid a Jewish doctor to sign my death certificate in Antwerp and I moved to be with my love in Warsaw. She is a good girl, Jadwiga. I know you will understand why I love her. She is a good woman. I wish now I would have moved to Warsaw a long time ago, but I never thought much about time and how it would end and what maybe I missed. I did my business and I worked hard. And I was good to the people I worked with, Theodore. You ask any of them. Josef Rimberg was a good man.

I would not want them to ask you what you thought. They might change their minds and think I'm not such a good guy. If maybe I moved a little faster, I could change your mind, but these doctors are quacks and I do not have a year anymore.

The other morning I woke up feeling sick and when I looked in the mirror my face was an orange color. This was not a healthy look. I went right over to Geneva on an airplane and got that money I took out of my business, which is not all the money but my Jadwiga and Paulina they got to eat too, and sent it to you. I sent you all those letters, too, that I meant to send you for Hanukkah, but I won't last to Hanukkah. You mostly got a lot of money. Don't think, Theodore, that I think I can bribe you to love me with money, but money does not hurt. And it is all I have got to give you, Theodore, because I have no time. My skin is orange because my liver won't cooperate anymore.

Do you know my best memory? Remember when me and you went to visit the Green Bay Packers summer training? David your brother was already too good to go around with his parents and wanted to meet girls in the park, so he and your mother stayed home. Me and you drove to Lambeau Field and saw the hall of fame, and I bought you that running back jersey. Terdell Middleton. I never liked his name. But he was a good running back. We stood out there with all the Packer fans and watched Lynn Dickey throw those passes to James Lofton. There is nothing so pretty as seeing real professionals play sports. Dickey threw those long passes that arched down the field, and Lofton leaped up and took those balls right from the sky. It was beautiful to watch. Nothing brings tears to my eyes. But thinking of those passes with my little boy Theodore holding my hand next to me. That does the job. Remember how Chester

Marcol kicked that ball so bad it bounced up to us on the sideline? I handed you the ball, and Chester let you run it back over to him. Nice man. There wasn't no cloud in the sky that day. Just bright, still, light. My best memory, Theodore. I remember it like it just happened. All that light.

You will understand soon how fast twenty-five years passes you by.

There have been only a few days when the world is light like that. The day when the Catholic boys and I went after that train. The day you were born. The day I came to Warsaw and saw your sister the first time. The day Brett Favre won the Super Bowl. I thought about you that day, even though it was the middle of the night in Antwerp. I turned on every light in the apartment and shouted out my window. I knew you were watching, too, Theodore. I knew you had your own children, and I worried so much about what I had done to you. But Brett Favre won it and I thought everything, Theodore, everything will turn out.

Twenty-five years, and I never thought we didn't have a good relationship. Now I am afraid of dying, I do not want to because now we will never sit down and have a good talk which is something we need. Your mother never wanted me to be in contact, which I gave her to pay her back for the trouble I caused. She would tell me how you are doing, which I thought was enough. But what can a mother really know? I should have stayed in your life. I never was afraid, but now I want to see you, Theodore. So I have a favor for you.

I am asking you to come to Warsaw immediately. This is the invitation I did not put in your inheritance. You get this letter, you come to Warsaw and we will talk. I would call your telephone, but I am afraid of your rejection and don't want it to be the last thing in my life. I prefer to think maybe we did have a good relationship all this time. It is a terrible chain, being afraid of dying and becoming a coward because I am afraid of what life might give me now that my liver stops working and my face is orange. We were friends, weren't we, Theodore?

Come to Warsaw. The address is on the envelope. You come. I will not be afraid anymore. We say goodbye. Then you take my ashes and put them at Lambeau Field. Jadwiga will not be happy with this, but you should see this jar she wants to put me in. It is not a good jar, and I do not want to be in a jar. She won't listen. I want to be with you in the Midwest.

You need to meet your sister even if I am gone. She has had bad luck but she's a good girl, she's typing this as I speak, not so well but we will fix it, and she could use a good brother like you.

You got money now. You get on a plane, okay, Theodore? We will talk about what we need to talk about.

With great love,

Your Father

Day Twelve:
Transcript 2

My dad was not a bad guy. At least, he didn't want to be a bad guy. That's something, I think.

Cranberry?

I wept when Cranberry showed up at the flat. I cried like a baby.

Cranberry carried all of the past with him . . . all of my reality before Poland . . . he somehow carried it . . . I only thought of Poland when I was in Poland.

Paulina, after she reread the letter, knew it was the right thing to do. Dad clearly didn't want to be in that bird vase. She got Pani Jadwiga to agree to take a trip to Krakow to see her cousins.

I felt very guilty, but it was necessary, Barry.

The whole thing was surreal. I walked them out to the car, knowing I was going to go. Paulina was just shaking. She whispered not to forget about her. They got in Paulina's car to drive south, and boom, Cranberry and I were off to America.

No, by that time I knew I wasn't in legal trouble. I mean I'd known for a couple of weeks. The U.S. embassy had finally called.

I would likely have left Warsaw after I found out Dad was dead. It was important that I believed I was in trouble.

Since I've been back, I've been in Milwaukee, bowling a lot.

No, I never went. I don't really like going to the doctor. I felt a little better after I stopped drinking, anyway.

I didn't call them. I thought about them a lot, of course . . . missed them while I was gone . . . you know when I was in jail in Poland. I don't know why I didn't contact them. Maybe I'm still an ass. I was afraid. I am going to see them now, you know? Nothing will stop me.

You mean why'd it take so long to get to Lambeau?

It wasn't my intention. I was trying to figure out how to get into the stadium. I definitely didn't intend to wait until August, but after looking and considering, I figured the only way I could do it was if there were a lot of people around, if I could somehow blend into the scenery. There was a training camp scrimmage scheduled in the stadium on the eighth. I saw that on the website. That's where I was headed when the accident happened.

Yes, I did have the note for Brett Favre Dad wanted me to deliver. It was written on the bottom of that last gooey letter Dad wrote.

It burned in the crash.

Dad told Brett Favre that the way he plays football is instructive. He said that you can't fear interceptions—you can't fear for your safety or you'll get hurt. You have to enjoy the ride, Brett! That kind of stuff. Pretty goofy.

Yes, I miss her a lot. My sister! We've talked on the phone several times throughout the summer. Pani was very very very angry. Out of control. Slapped at Paulina, threatened to throw her out of the apartment. Not good.

Oh, she calmed down eventually. I spoke with her on the phone in July. She understands English, you know.

Yes, of course I miss Paulina. I already said that.

What are you smiling about?

What do you mean nothing?

Well, anyway, that's pretty much the story. I've been in
Wisconsin ever since May, waiting for football season. I was on
my way to the stadium when it all exploded.

Nope. I haven't written a journal entry or letter since Kristallnacht.

Why are you smiling like that, Barry?

Paulina?

When? Into Green Bay? When?

Did you arrange this?

Charlie?

Barry, when?

You are—you really, really are—the most beautiful priest I have
ever met. I know. I know. But you still are. You are, Barry.

Section IV

Green Bay

Letter 58
Letter left at front desk of St. Vincent's Care Center, Green Bay, WI
August 22, 2005

Dear Father Barry,

Watch out. I have a pen in my hand. I haven't written anything in nine months other than bowling scores and phone numbers, but now in my hand is a pen you left behind after we talked yesterday. The pen is advertising St. Vincent Catholic Church's summer schedule. "Our services are prayer conditioned." Did someone from the diocese write that?

Speaking of Saint Vincent, I read about him in *Life of the Saints,* a large beaten book that sits next to the television in the common room here. Saint Vincent de Paul, the book said, loved everyone: poor, rich, crazy, ignorant, sweet. Saint Vincent, as you probably know, cared for everyone and asked everyone to be humble and to take special care of the sick and the sad.

All of Green Bay was like Saint Vincent last night.

I felt very loved up there at the accident site, on the embankment, where thin threads of light dance off the burnt pavement when it gets dark. Charlie, my son, nuzzled his head into my chest as the sky darkened, and people surrounded me to thank me for my actions. I'm glad my right arm isn't in a cast, so I could hug Charlie to me.

You asked me what changed between the time Charlie arrived on the bus from Minneapolis, so sullen and cold, and the time we drove out to the accident site, when he was better. I didn't want to answer in front of Charlie; I didn't want to embarrass him. You were right, something changed. But nothing is fixed.

When me and Charlie were alone in my room, after Faye left to get Paulina, I stood up from the bed and said to him, "Oh

man, there you are. You're here. It is so good to see you, Charlie."
I had tears in my eyes. My voice wavered.

Charlie didn't respond. He looked out the window and his eyes began to tear up.

I said, "You're mad. You should be angry. I'm so sorry." I moved to hug him, and he shoved me back onto my bed.

"You are a shit-bag dad," he shouted. "I hate you."

I sat there on my bed for a moment, staring at his face that just said shit, his little-boy face, red and swollen with anger. He pushed me onto this bed, Father B., where for the last two weeks I've had to think so hard about what I've done, which hasn't been a great deal of fun. And I nodded, and I said, "Charlie, I have been a terrible, horrible shit-bag dad. I know."

"You're lucky I'm even here. Mom made me come."

"I'm so sorry. I'm so lucky you're here. I don't deserve such a good son."

"You're an asshole dad," Charlie sobbed.

"Asshole dad?" I asked.

"Yes," he said.

This is strong language, Father Barry. It hurt. But I told him he was right, and that his language didn't go far enough. I told him we'd have to come up with much worse language to cover what kind of dad I've actually been because *asshole* and *shit bag* don't really do the matter justice. Charlie listened. I caught his attention. He's been working as an extra at the Guthrie Theater this year while I've been gone. Apparently he's learned new ways of expressing himself. He found more terrible language to describe me. He used lots of new words.

It helped Charlie to express himself as truthfully as he could. By the time Faye returned from the airport with Paulina, Charlie was in the mood to hug everyone. He hugged Paulina, which made her cry, and Faye, who apparently cries more often than not. And I cried, too, because what am I going to do with all of this?

This morning, after everything last night, I was really emotional, and I sat Charlie down in the chairs where you and I sit to talk. I looked into his eyes, and I asked him to forgive me.

He smiled and said, "No." Then he laughed. Then he went to the nurses' station to get a donut. He returned with an extra donut and gave it to me. Then we watched cartoons.

Father Barry, I can't make up for what I've done. Still, Charlie loves me. He brought me a donut. I don't necessarily deserve to be forgiven, you know? But I think we're going to be okay. He wants to be my son. Would I have forgiven my father if given the chance? I don't know. I still love him. I think I understand him, and if I had a chance to talk to Dad, I would tell him that I understand. Maybe *forgiveness* is an empty word. Maybe acceptance is all there is. Chances are Dad would've screwed up again if he had lived. Would I have brought him a donut? Probably.

What a strange night.

From watching television, I didn't imagine the accident site correctly. Yes, there were hundreds of people, a mob. But driving up and seeing those people against the backdrop of a flat landscape that goes on forever was a little underwhelming. People are so small and the sky is enormous and the browns and grays of the earth and pavement stretch away forever. TV puts everything in a box, intensifies it all, but the land goes on and on.

It wasn't until we moved into the crowd that I felt the intensity. We were guided in by the police and people pushed toward me to get a look. They smiled and waved and shook my hand. The sun began to set. So many in the crowd held candles, and the light pooled in the darkening air, which began to create a sense of boundary from the enormous sky. We arrived at the edge of the downed overpass and I could see people in their shorts and Packer T-shirts lined up down the highway and on the opposite embankment, so many with lit candles, like All Souls'

Day in Poland, the whole scene bathed in candlelight. And the sun went down and the air rose.

And I saw it. Heat from the departed sun rose off the pavement. I saw it. Quiet Green Bay whispered and prayed, and Charlie nuzzled into me, and Paulina stared down at the highway, then turned toward me, her mouth open, because she couldn't understand what we were seeing: wisps of light, strings of lit dust lifting from the burnt pavement and twisting in the air, organizing and breaking, then reconfiguring, rising up. I don't know, Father Barry.

You asked, after, what I made of it all, seeing the scene. I have a hard time believing I have anything to say about anything. I'm aware, after reading through the notebooks with you, that I am a huge fool. But before the letters, Father, I never said anything to anybody. Even if I never sent a single one of those letters and never intended to send them and even if I'm crazy, when I began to write them, I was trying to communicate something, wasn't I?

Dad was trying, too, it seems.

Okay. Listen. I think I've seen it before. I think the light is from Dublin and Julia, and from Paris in the Seine, and it was in Antwerp in the park, and I saw candlelight mix with that kind of light in the Polish cemetery. It might be the light my dad saw the day he and his Catholic brothers attacked the train and released a hundred and fifty people who were bound for Auschwitz. If I've seen it, millions of people have seen it in a million different ways, and I don't know what it is. It might be nothing at all or it might be something. I think it's something.

"What do you make of all this?" you asked. I couldn't answer and maybe I shouldn't, but I'm going to.

Father Barry, I'm sorry. I didn't see the Virgin Mary down there where the bus crashed and the overpass collapsed. But I understand why you might see her, why Catholics see her. The light is amazing. And there is this astonishing thing that happened. If an astonishing thing is a miracle, that was my miracle . . . and the Virgin Mary is associated with miracles. Maybe that light is her and I simply don't have the background to recognize her. Maybe Mary showed up to mark the spot. But I didn't see her.

I saw dust that gathered light and rose on the air from the burnt pavement, dust that rose and danced.

What do I make of all this? My first inclination is to shrug and to believe the guy on CNN who said, "It's marvelous to see, but come on. The light is caused by the chemicals the fire department used to douse the fire. The foam left a dust, and the dust rises on heat from the pavement, and it's being illuminated by man-made sources of light." Yes. Sounds right. You know, Dad's ashes are also mixed up with that foam dust. Maybe his earthly remains are incandescent. He was quite a guy.

But my inclinations don't stop with that first one. My second inclination is to think of Van Gogh's painting *Starry Night*. My third inclination is to think of Julia Hilfgott in a bubble of light by an Irish cemetery. My fourth inclination is to see my sister illuminated as a little girl in my dreams, saving me. My fifth inclination is to remember. I remember now, Father Barry. I remember hitting the tour bus after it veered and crashed into the overpass in front of me. I remember exploding into the side of the bus. I remember opening my eyes, the airbag deflating, dust from my father's bird vase thick in the air. I remember thinking, "What just happened?" I remember kicking the door out, sliding out of the luggage hold of the bus, running away then stopping, hearing the roar of fires and screams behind me. I remember turning back to the bus, thinking, "This is a disaster." And I remember charging into the fires to free the people on the bus, seeing slabs of concrete from the overpass that had buckled when the bus hit its support blocking the door to the bus, screams from the bus and faces pressed against glass. I remember crying to them, "I can't get to you." I remember climbing the remains of the overpass and finding a pick-up truck crashed and empty on it (the driver had apparently already run). I remember rolling the pick-up truck off to the right, rolling it over the edge of the buckled lane where it dropped ten feet onto its side (I hoped getting the truck off the overpass would somehow help me move the slabs that blocked the bus door, which was wishful thinking, except . . .). When the truck hit the pavement, it exploded. The explosion shot me into the air, and for a moment I had this slow, clear view of Lambeau Field and I knew I had to die, knew it was time, and I laughed because I thought, "Oh, now that I don't want to die, this is what I get?" And then I was amazed because I knew I wanted to live. I fell to the earth screaming. Rebar saved me. I fell onto hot bands of metal that bent with my weight, slowed me. For a moment I hung there, yards from the ground, my back searing, and I cried out in pain, but mostly in celebration. I swore with words Charlie hasn't even dreamed of. I broke my arm as I twisted out of the metal and I cried, "Fuck you, arm!" And I looked up and saw the bus door. The exploding pick-up truck had moved the bus, cleared most of the cement in front of its door. I ran to the door, shoved and kicked the remaining blocks of concrete, and opened the door, and people tumbled down the stairs and out, shoving into me, screaming. I climbed into the bus, crawled along the floor, pulled people out from under crumpled seats with my good arm. People dragged their children and parents out around me. The machine roar of the fire swallowed their cries. Fire climbed the windows. Heavy smoke billowed and exploded, carrying burning fabric. "I'm not going to die," I shouted at people who escaped. Finally, I pulled a girl who seemed dead out from under a seat. I pinched her to me, dragged her toward the door, past the bus driver, his mouth open, dead eyes open—a heart attack, I heard, that caused the whole accident in the first place. I said sorry. And then I dragged this girl down the stairs, tripping on her dead legs, out of the bus. People were screaming at me as we emerged from the smoke, heading toward the cars and the crowd, away from the bus.

I think the bus exploded then. I remember a deafening sound and nothing else until your blurry face, backlit from a window, Father Barry. We were in the hospital. You bent over me. You said, "Mr. Rimberg. The Lord has blessed you." You made me laugh.

Later I remember waking and wondering where I'd put my father's ashes. I couldn't remember, but knew my loss had something to do with the cards and phone calls from families and the visit from the family of some girl who was in stable condition somewhere else in the hospital. And you were in my room wanting to talk, and I felt broken everywhere, and groggy, and confused. I was most definitely alive, even though I had the sense I shouldn't be so lucky.

And what did we talk about when we sat together? You had somehow gotten your hands on my notebooks. We talked about this exhausting, ridiculous year I've had, this year spawned from my utter inability to live decently.

There are things I want to say. They grew during the time we've been together. I wasn't sure I wanted to say these things, Father Barry. I wasn't sure of them. But having Charlie here and Paulina, having seen what I saw last night—I have to give voice to these things.

I am a complete idiot, a narcissist, a navel gazer, and a philanderer. I am humbled and culpable. But I am happy I was suicidal. I am delighted I saw ghosts. I believe my dad talked to me after he died. I saw my little sister in my dreams before I knew she existed. I saved a busload of goddamn Packer fans from death. I am a father. This is all real and right and I am not ashamed. Life is a complete disaster. It is horrible and ridiculous.

I am so lucky to have this chance. Most people aren't so lucky. They should pay better attention.

That's what I have to say.

Now I'm going to pull Charlie from watching TV in the common room. We're going to meet Faye and Paulina at the Perkins across the parking lot for some breakfast (even though my smarty-pants son says he doesn't want to eat at a chain restaurant). I will buy breakfast for all of them, anything they want, because I love these people.

Later today, Faye is driving us to Minneapolis so Paulina can meet my daughters. I'm going to hug them and take all the abuse and anger they've got, because I deserve it. And then I'm going to tell them some amazing stories. And then what? I'm going to love my kids and they're going to know it. I'll go from there.

Sound like a plan? I hope so, because that's all I got.

Thank you so much for what you've done, Father Barry. Really. Thank you.

T.

Acknowledgments

First, Lindsey Moore is a great editor. Lindsey is perceptive and creative and I can't thank her enough for taking a chance on this book. Thank you to my great agent, Jim McCarthy, who is calm when I am not. My Lit6 pals? Steph Ash, Brady Bergeson, and Sam Osterhout? I owe you so much. In fact, thank you to the whole EARS crew: Dave Salmela, Jenny Adams, Kurt Froehlich, Paul D. Dickenson, Mike Brady, Peter Robelia, Tony Mogelson, Kevin Riach, and Quillan Roe. To the web team: Andy Sturdevant and Karen Kopacz. Thank you to my Hamline University peers who had an impact on this book: Shannon Schenck, Susan Montag, Scott Wisgerhof, Dave Oppegaard, Sandy Beach, and Alison Morse (more great friends here than I can mention). Thank you to Hamline teachers: Deborah Keenan, Mary Rockcastle, and, especially, Sheila O'Connor. I am forever indebted to the Hamline program. I would be remiss if I didn't thank Jen and Colin Plese, Jason Jones, Duane McLaughlin, and Brad Thayer, all of whom are brilliant and all of whom retarded my ability to function normally at exactly the right moment. Thank you to URPL stars Branden Born and Jerry Kaufman. And, of course, to Marty McGinley, Todd Louthain, Chris Bierbrauer, and the whole Platteville crew. Thanks to George Jonas and Mary Healy Jonas. Thanks to Jason Oates. Thanks to my incredible, supportive, and talented family (so much to Vovo, Michael Zahler, Jonathan Herbach, Yol and Steve, Marisa, and Grandma Elinor). Thanks to Amy Naughton. And, finally, thank you to my beautiful kids, Leo and Mira, who are seemingly not nonplussed at having a slightly weird dad. I love you so much.